JF
THE DONU...
RIGGED RISING

Rigged Rising, Donut Mystery 47
Copyright © 2020 by Jessica Beck
All rights reserved.
First edition: 2020

No part of this book may be reproduced, scanned, or distributed in any printed or electronic form without permission. Please do not participate in or encourage piracy of copyrighted materials in violation of the author's rights. This is a work of fiction. Names, characters, places, and incidents either are the product of the author's imagination or are used fictitiously, and any resemblance to actual persons, living or dead, business establishments, events, or locales is entirely coincidental.

Recipes included in this book are to be recreated at the reader's own risk. The author is not responsible for any damage, medical or otherwise, created as a result of reproducing these recipes. It is the responsibility of the reader to ensure that none of the ingredients are detrimental to their health, and the author will not be held liable in any way for any problems that might arise from following the included recipes.

The First Time Ever Published!
The 47th Donut Mystery
RIGGED RISING

Jessica Beck is the *New York Times* Bestselling Author of the Donut Mysteries, the Cast Iron Cooking Mysteries, the Classic Diner Mysteries, the Ghost Cat Cozy Mysteries, and more.

THERE'S A MAYORAL ELECTION in April Springs, North Carolina, and just as George Morris discovers that he's been unseated by rival Lily Hamilton, the new mayor-elect winds up dead! A great many fingers point toward George as the main suspect in the murder, so Suzanne and her stepfather, Phillip, must dive into the case to clear their friend's name and, in doing so, find the real killer.

To you all, my dear readers, thank you for coming along for the ride. And to P and E, both simply the best!

Chapter 1

"I'M SORRY, MR. MAYOR. You were winning the election until we got down to the last batch of ballots, but in the end, it just wasn't enough," Nathan Billings—our new head of the April Springs Board of Elections—said as we all stood around the city hall basement, waiting for the election results. "In the end, you lost by 53 votes. The threshold for a formal challenge is 50, so I'm afraid it's all over. If it's any consolation, you ran a good race."

"I appreciate you saying that, Nathan," George said gamely. "The truth is that Lily beat me fair and square."

"I wish everyone took defeat so gracefully. Anyway, I thought you had the right to hear it directly from me first. Now if you'll excuse me, I need to find mayor-elect Hamilton and have her sign some paperwork. Until she does that, you're still the mayor." I saw Nathan stop and have a quick word with Max, my ex-husband. I didn't realize that they even knew each other, but that was the way it was with small towns. There were connections within connections, and *nobody* knew *every* story. Maybe that was what kept life interesting.

"Mayor in name only," George said with a shrug as the head of the board of elections left in search of our new mayor. It had been a hard-fought campaign, but ultimately, we'd come up just a little short. I'd helped run the mayor's campaign out of my donut shop, and it felt as though every moment I hadn't been making or selling donuts in the past three weeks, I'd been trying to get votes for my friend.

George Morris looked from me to Momma, then Jake, and finally, Grace. "Folks, I'm sorry I let you all down. You campaigned hard for me, and I appreciate it. I'm just upset that I wasn't worthy of your efforts in the end."

I hugged George fiercely. "Don't you dare believe that for one instant. You were worth every second. Hey, you heard the man. It went down to the wire. You can hold your head up, proud not only for the way you ran for reelection, but for the way you held office, too."

Momma stepped forward after I released the mayor and hugged him, too. "George, I know that in the beginning, I shanghaied you into taking the job, but to my delight, you managed to exceed even my already-high expectations. You were a credit to your office."

"Thanks, Dot," he said. "I appreciate that."

"What are you going to do now?" Jake asked him.

He didn't even have to think about his answer. "I want to finish the job we started on my lake house. What do you say? Are you up for it? I know you're running a consulting business these days for outside law enforcement agencies, but if you have any gaps in your schedule, I'd love to have you work with me."

"As a matter of fact, I've got the next three weeks free before my next job," Jake said with a grin. I'd expected my husband to be more in demand as a former state police investigator, but apparently it took time for people to come around. "Should we go over and get started on it right now? Tearing out a wall or two might do you some good tonight. After all, there's nothing like a sledgehammer in your hands to work out some of your aggression."

George laughed. "As tempting as that sounds, I've got to hang around and be the gracious loser tonight. Lily deserves that much." He looked around the room. "Where is she, anyway? I figured she'd be celebrating like crazy after beating me."

"Speaking of folks who are absent, where's Zinnia?" I asked as I looked around the room as well. George had been dating the recluse for several months now, though it would have been difficult to prove it by most of the folks in April Springs. Zinnia liked to keep to herself, an odd companion for such a public figure as a mayor, but it seemed to work for them, at least according to George.

"She's not coming," the mayor said with the hint of a frown.

"What's wrong? Is there trouble in paradise?" Grace asked him gently.

"I guess you could say that. The second Zinnia realized that I was serious about running for reelection, she dumped me," George said matter-of-factly.

"Now that you've lost the election, surely you two can work things out," Momma said.

"Honestly, I don't want to," he answered. "*This* has become who I am. I'm thinking about running for town council and seeing life from the other side of the mayor's desk. Politics has kind of gotten into my blood." He grinned as he added that last part. "I never would have believed it."

"Me either," I said with a smile. "But since you're not dating anyone at the moment, I know for a fact that Angelica DeAngelis would go out with you in a heartbeat if you asked her."

"Suzanne Hart, the man just lost his girlfriend *and* his job," Momma scolded me. "Give him some time to mourn both."

"I'm just saying, he couldn't do any better than Angelica," I countered.

"I'm not about to disagree with you, but it's none of your business," Momma chastised me.

"I disagree. He's my friend, and that *makes* it my business, Momma," I replied. "Isn't that right, George?"

"What? I'm sorry; I didn't hear that last part. Why is Chief Grant heading over here? He looks upset about something."

"It's probably because he's not all that crazy about his new boss," Grace said. She and the chief of police had been dating for some time, but neither one of them seemed to be in all that big a rush to get married.

"Maybe you're right," the mayor said, but it was clear that he didn't believe it.

"Mayor, Jake, would you two mind coming with me for a few minutes?" Chief Grant asked the moment he approached us. "Sorry, ladies, but I won't keep them long."

"What's going on, Stephen?" Grace asked. If I'd posed the same question, there would have been little hope of him answering, but he wasn't about to brush off his fiancée's query.

"Something's happened," Chief Grant said softly, "but I'm not ready to make a formal announcement just yet."

"What is it, Chief?" the mayor asked. "If it's really that important, shouldn't we get Lily Hamilton in on this, too?"

"That's the thing," Chief Grant said gently as he looked around the room. "Lily's been murdered."

Chapter 2

"MURDERED?" I ASKED, fighting to keep my voice down. "How? When did it happen? Who else knows? Do you have any idea who did it?" The questions shot out of me as though they were captive birds trying to escape their cages.

"Slow down. It's way too early to answer most of those questions right now," the chief said.

"I need to come with you, too," I said.

"Suzanne, I know that you have a knack for this sort of thing, but I'm trying to keep this information contained as long as I can," he replied.

"That's what makes this so perfect. I have the added bonus of already knowing about it myself. You can trust me. I'll stay out of your way," I promised.

"She might be able to help," Jake interjected on my behalf.

"I think so, too," George added.

It warmed my heart to have them back me up, and the chief clearly didn't want to stand there and argue about it. "Fine. How about the two of you?" he asked Grace and Momma. "Do you want to tag along, too?"

My mother answered quickly, "No thank you."

"How about you, Grace?"

"I'll hang around here and try to deflect any suspicions if people start getting nosy," she said. I knew Grace was looking out for both her fiancé and me, and I appreciated it very much.

"Come on, then," he said as he gestured toward the three of us he'd agreed to let go with him. "It happened out back."

We followed the police chief out of the basement and made our way upstairs to the rear exit. The first floor was City Hall proper, and I saw George glance up the stairs toward his office, or at least what used to be his office. "Does this mean that you're still the mayor?" I asked him.

"Legally maybe, but not in spirit. It's pretty clear from the results that folks around here didn't want me," George said calmly. "I can't imagine trying to serve without any kind of mandate, especially when someone killed the real winner."

"Let's not worry about that just yet. We'll talk about it later," I said, cutting him off before he could talk himself into walking away from the job forever. In my opinion, we needed George at the helm more than ever now that Lily was dead. It may have seemed a little too quick to start thinking about who was going to run things so soon after the poor woman's murder, but April Springs *needed* someone in charge. I couldn't imagine how things would be without any mayor at all, and I didn't want to.

The three of us followed Chief Grant outside and around the back. The police station/jail was close, but instead of leading us toward it, he moved around the building until we could see the back of The Last Page, our town's independent bookstore.

At first I couldn't see the mayor-elect's body, but it was easy enough to spot Officer Darby Jones standing near what turned out to be the corpse. Darby studied us each in turn before he spoke. "That's quite a crowd you've got there, Chief."

"Maybe so, but it's your job to make sure that it doesn't get any bigger," Chief Grant said curtly. "Go stand at the exit of city hall. No one comes in or goes out unless they have my express permission. Got that?"

He snapped alert. "Yes, sir."

"Then do it."

Once he was gone, Jake asked, "Problems with your staff?"

"Nothing I can't handle," Chief Grant answered. He took out a small handheld flashlight and played it over the body.

I wasn't sure I was ready to look at a fresh corpse, but I didn't really have much choice.

After all, I'd practically begged to be included, so I couldn't look away now.

Lily was lying on her stomach, facing toward us. Her head was canted to one side, and I could see that her eyes were still open, as though she was staring at the grass in front of her face.

The murder weapon wasn't far away.

It was one of the ballot boxes we used for our elections, an old-fashioned system that had worked fine for April Springs for a hundred years. Evidently someone had lifted it over their head and brought it crashing down onto Lily's skull.

It must have killed her instantly.

"Is the ballot box empty?" I asked out of curiosity. I wasn't sure why, but it had been the first thing that had popped into my mind.

"Does that really matter at a time like this, Suzanne?" the chief asked.

"Maybe not, but don't you want to know, too?"

He shrugged. "Right now I don't care. Mr. Mayor, I'd like you to go back inside and make the announcement. They'll take it better if it's coming from you, and I need to stay here and work the crime scene. Jake, do you mind hanging around?"

"Not at all," my husband said.

"What would you like me to do?" I asked him.

"Go with the mayor," the chief said as he eyed our suddenly unsteady head of state.

I glanced at George, and he definitely looked taken aback by what had happened. Though he had been a seasoned police officer himself once upon a time, this had clearly hit too close to home for him.

I nodded. "Come on, Mr. Mayor."

"Don't call me that," George snapped at me. Instantly, he must have realized how he'd sounded. "I'm sorry, Suzanne. I lost the title and the job tonight, and I surely don't want to keep serving this way."

"Maybe not, but for the moment, you're all that we've got, and we need you," I said as I took his arm in mine. "Come on. Let's get this over with."

"Fine, but I'm not staying in office a second longer after this mess is all straightened out," George insisted.

"Nobody's asking you to," I said. I turned to the chief. "You know everyone's going to panic when they hear the news and want to get out of there, right?"

"They can leave, but it's going to be in an orderly fashion. I'll have three officers standing by the door, taking names and checking IDs. Until we know more, that's going to be the best that we can do."

"That sounds like a good plan," I said as I glanced over at Jake.

My husband nodded, and then he pulled out a pair of latex gloves from his back pocket, knelt down by the body, and studied it as he played the beam of his small flashlight over Lily Hamilton. Jake must have been one heck of a Boy Scout, because he *always* seemed to be prepared for just about any emergency.

Most days, I was lucky if I knew where my car keys were.

That was what made us such a great team, though. Jake was methodical, while I was more intuitive. Between the two of us, there wasn't *anything* we couldn't tackle.

I just hoped we were up for investigating this murder.

Our friend, the mayor, needed us, and I had a feeling that the chief wouldn't mind us nosing around the investigation this time.

After all, this case needed to be solved, and fast, before higher authorities stepped in and took it away from us all.

"George, you look a little shaken up by what happened to Lily. Are you going to be okay?" I asked him softly.

"I'm fine, Suzanne. The truth is that Lily and I dated a few times, but it was quite a while ago. I'm just trying to figure out why someone would kill her."

"I'm sure she's made her share of enemies over the years," I said. "How could she not? She was a stubborn woman used to getting her own way, and when she didn't, she wasn't above going after anybody that got in her sights." I felt bad about speaking ill of the dead, but I'd have to get over that. This was the time for the truth, no matter how raw it might seem. Lily was now the victim, not someone who came in rarely to get donuts at my shop. She deserved justice, and if finding her killer also cleared my friend's name, then so much the better. "Have you got any ideas about possible suspects?"

"A few, but I can't think about them right now," George said. "I have to tell everyone that Lily's dead. I need to focus on that."

George nodded to the officers now stationed at the exit, and we walked back inside. As we entered the basement where we'd so recently been awaiting the election results, we were suddenly inundated by people wanting to know where the mayor-elect was hiding.

I walked George to the steps that led up to the stage. "This is as far as I can go. You can do this, George."

"Thanks, Suzanne."

He approached the microphone and was immediately assaulted with questions from the audience, not the least insistent of which was Ray Blake, owner of our local newspaper and generally an all-around pain in the rump to anyone who got between him and a story. George waited them all out though, and finally the murmurs died down so he could speak.

"I'm afraid this isn't going to be the concession speech that some of you were hoping for," he led off with. He clearly hadn't meant it to be funny, but there were a few chuckles from the crowd, no doubt coming from some of the folks who had voted for him. "What I mean to say is that something has happened tonight that has made this night a tragedy for us all instead of a victory for one."

The recently defeated mayor took a deep breath, and then he announced sadly, "I'm sorry to announce that Lily Hamilton is dead."

The room exploded the moment after his announcement once everyone realized that he was serious, and I had to block Ray from leaping up the steps to attack George with questions face to face.

It was going to be a long night for all of us, and worse yet, I had to get up much earlier than anyone should ever have to and make donuts in the morning.

It was just part of my job, but at that point, I would have gladly traded it for any number of occupations that would have allowed me to defend my friend from the onslaught he was now facing and still get a little sleep in the process.

"George, you need to get off the stage right now," I insisted as I tugged at his jacket. "You aren't holding a press conference. You've done what the police chief asked you to do. There's nothing more you can do."

"You're right, Suzanne," he said as he let me lead him away.

Folks were still shouting questions at the poor man, but there wasn't much more he knew, so he couldn't exactly answer them. Being a former cop himself, he knew not to disclose any real information, such as the murder weapon and the state the victim had been found in, so that made it even tougher.

Ray Blake got in one last shot, though. "Since you were defeated in the general election, are you still planning on surrendering your office, *Mr.* Morris?" The lack of the mayor's title was noticeable.

"Don't answer him, George," I said softly. "He's baiting you."

Evidently Ray heard it anyway. "What are *you* trying to hide, Suzanne?"

"Go away, Ray," I said firmly. I wanted to say much more to him than that, but his daughter and his wife worked for me, and I couldn't afford to alienate them both, no matter how much provocation Ray gave me.

"You wish," he said, almost licking his lips in anticipation of the story he was about to write, whether he had the facts or not.

I firmly kept my mouth shut, and once we were through the line of folks giving their names and addresses to the police officers on site, I told the mayor, "That was even more brutal than I thought it was going to be."

"I don't blame them. They deserve answers," George said.

"Even Ray Blake?" I asked with a hint of a smile.

"Yes, even Ray Blake."

"You can't quit, George," I said resolutely as my smile vanished. It was time to settle this before he talked himself into walking away. "We *need* you."

"Suzanne, you heard Nathan Billings. I lost the election."

"I'm not so sure about that," I said.

He looked at me oddly. "What are you talking about?"

"I keep wondering if anyone has looked *inside* the murder weapon," I said softly. "For all we know, there could still be unrecorded ballots in there. You might not have lost after all."

"I don't care," George said flatly. "If it was that close, I don't want the job."

He seemed thoroughly fed up with the situation, and I couldn't say that I blamed him. If I were in his shoes, would I fight so hard to retain a job that so many voters didn't want me to perform? I wasn't sure, but I knew one thing. George was no quitter. At least I hoped that was still the case.

"Promise me one thing, as my friend," I said.

"What is it? I need to know what you're asking before I agree to anything," he replied.

"Don't make any decisions tonight. If you feel the same way in the morning, we can talk about it then, but for the moment, at least give us a *little* stability in the town's top job. Is that too much to ask of an old friend?"

"I guess I could do that, for you," George admitted. I could swear that I saw him start limping slightly as he headed back to the crime scene. A very long time ago, ages before George had entered politics, he'd worked with me to help me solve cases. One of our suspects had run him down with her car. She'd tried to kill him, and only his quick reflexes had saved his life. Every now and then, that ghostly limp would come back, mostly during times when George seemed troubled and stressed. I felt guilty every time I saw it, knowing that I'd been the one who had sent him on that fateful mission, and that he very well could have died from that impact instead of surviving and going on to be our mayor.

Chapter 3

GEORGE AND I FOUND Jake and the police chief at the scene in deep conversation. As they saw us approach, Chief Grant asked, "How did it go, Mr. Mayor?"

"It was a feeding frenzy, but George managed to hold his own," I said as I patted my friend's shoulder before he could dispute his title yet again.

"I don't know about that," George piped in. "I couldn't tell them anything other than the fact that Lily was dead, and they started getting aggressive and looking for an explanation. I couldn't even blame them. I want to know what happened myself."

"I know there wasn't much doubt before, but the ballot box was definitely the murder weapon," the chief said. "The coroner confirmed it, so I have it locked up in the trunk of my squad car."

"Did you at least check it for ballots?" I asked.

"Suzanne, it hardly matters at this point. The way I see it, George just got another full term in office," the police chief said.

"That's where you're wrong," the mayor, at least for now, said. "Suzanne made me promise not to do anything rash tonight, or to make any decisions until morning, but right now I can't imagine staying in office even one more day."

I thought about another incentive that might make George change his mind. "Does that mean that you're going to let Travis Johnson just have your job?" The mayor and Travis went way back, and all of their history was bad. They'd butted heads back when George had been a cop and Travis had opened his first dry cleaner, and the bad blood had just gotten worse and worse every year. Travis now owned four dry cleaners in the general area, and he also had a stake in a few other ventures as well. He also happened to be involved heavily in our local politics, something that the mayor had complained about in the past on more than one occasion.

"I don't know about that," George said.

"Isn't he the head of the city council?" I asked. "The way I understand it, if you walk away, he steps in and takes over." I knew that was true, even though I'd never seen it happen in my lifetime. Mrs. Forbush, my junior high school civics teacher, had lectured on and on about our local government, including the succession plan in case something happened to our sitting mayor.

"How could you possibly know that?" Jake asked me, clearly surprised by another piece of my esoteric, and usually rather useless, knowledge.

"Mrs. Forbush," the chief and George both said at the same time.

"I can understand Chief Grant having her in school, but was she really teaching when *you* were a kid, too?" I asked George incredulously.

"As a matter of fact, she wasn't all that much older than I was at the time. She did her student teaching here in town, and I had her during her very first semester," George explained. "Besides, I'm not *that* old."

"Absolutely. You're still a young pup as far as I'm concerned," I lied with a smile as I patted his arm, and then I turned to the chief. "May I at least inspect the ballot box to see if there are any votes in there that haven't been counted yet?"

"We need to leave that to the head of the Board of Elections," the chief said, "but I see your point," he added quickly before I could protest further. Turning to one of his officers, he said, "Get me Nathan Billings out here on the double."

"What if he's already gone?" the chief's underling asked.

"Then find him," the chief snapped, and then in a softer tone of voice, he added, "but he's going to be here. This is his Super Bowl and Christmas all rolled into one. He's not going anywhere."

"I'll go get him," the officer said.

"How well do you know Nathan?" I asked the chief after his underling left.

"We went to high school together," Chief Grant explained. "He was the head of the audiovisual club, the computer club, the theater club, and the chess club. We all thought he'd get out of April Springs the first chance he got, but he couldn't afford college, and he had no one to help him pay for it. His mother died young, and his father was a drunk."

"That's tough, but there are other ways to get a degree," I said.

"Yeah, but Nathan had other obligations he couldn't walk away from," the chief said.

I was hoping for more of an explanation when the man himself walked up. I had no idea if he knew that we'd just been talking about him, but I felt guilty nonetheless. He asked pointedly, "What is it, Chief? I'm checking the votes we've gotten to be sure our tally stands, even though I fear it's a moot point." He glanced at George and then frowned. "I'm sorry, Mr. Mayor, but there's no doubt in my mind that our original tally is correct."

"Not if you didn't count all of the ballots that were cast in the election," I said.

Nathan looked at me and shook his head. "I don't know what you're talking about, Ms. Hart. We counted every last vote."

"Including the ones still in the ballot box that's sitting in the trunk of the chief's squad car even as we speak?" I asked him.

"What? I don't believe it. The ballot boxes have all been accounted for." The man seemed absolutely stunned that it could be within the realm of possibility that he could have missed some votes.

"I'd count them again if I were you. You seem to be one short," the chief said as he led the head of elections, and all of us, toward his trunk. After Chief Grant popped open the trunk lid, he put on a pair of rubber gloves and removed the box from the large bag he'd secured it in.

I could see that it was still locked, so no one had tampered with it, at least as far as I could tell.

"Do you have a key to this thing so we can check it out?" he asked Nathan.

"It's right here," Nathan Billings said as he moved to open the box himself.

"Not so fast. I'll do that, if you don't mind," the chief said. It was clear the two men had some kind of history, but I found myself hoping that they'd forget about it for the moment. After all, we had more important issues to deal with than childhood rivalries from long ago.

After all, we still had a dead body on our hands, and so far, none of us had any idea who had bashed Lily Hamilton over the head with a ballot box.

"Chief, if I'm going to certify this election, *I* have to be the one who removes them *myself*." It was clear that Nathan Billings was standing on the duties of his office, but it was just as obvious that the chief wasn't going to budge.

Jake spoke up. "Chief Grant, did you get all of the fingerprints, photos, and video of the murder weapon that you needed?"

"You know I did. You were standing right there when my guys did it."

"*I* know that, but I wanted to be sure that *you* remembered it. I realize that this is unorthodox, but an election might be at stake here."

"You're right," Chief Grant said with a shrug. He moved back a step and handed Nathan a fresh pair of gloves.

"What am I supposed to do with those?" the head of the Board of Elections asked.

"Put them on," Chief Grant said, failing to hide the hint of irritation in his voice.

"Of course," Nathan said.

After he'd donned the gloves he'd been given, the chief said, "Open the lock, remove it from the hasp, and then stand back. We need to record this, and then we need to examine the contents, if any, of the ballot box."

"Then these votes won't be counted," Nathan Billings said with a hint of resignation in his voice. That was the way it was with some people. The less power they had, the more they tried to use it as a club to get their way.

"You can be with me the entire time," the chief explained. "We won't do anything unless you're watching us. Once we go through anything that's inside, we'll turn the ballots over to you, if there are any. Surely that has to be good enough."

"Yes, I suppose that should be sufficient," Nathan said. Clearly he was just as eager as the rest of us to see what was inside the ballot box.

Would it be more votes for George, maybe even enough to put him over the top, or would it be full of votes for Lily Hamilton, rubbing the defeat in even more? Then again, it could be empty, and things would stand just as they were.

I found myself holding my breath as the chief leaned forward, took the now-open lock off the hasp securing the box's lid, and swung the ballot box's door lid open for all of us to see what, if anything, was inside.

Chapter 4

"IT'S STUFFED *full* of ballots," I said, stating the obvious. "I'm guessing that *none* of these made your count," I said to Nathan.

I wasn't trying to rub it in, but his reaction told me that I'd hit him below the belt. "This is extraordinary. I won't be able to certify the election now no matter who the winner is. *Anyone* could have stuffed this box full of ballots for either candidate without us even knowing about it."

"I think it's a moot point, anyway," the police chief said. "George Morris is our mayor until we get this mess straightened out."

"I'm still not so sure about that," the mayor said.

"At least let us count the votes they missed, Mayor," Jake said. "If you really did win, don't the people deserve to have you as their mayor?"

"And if Lily *still* wins?" George asked.

"We'll burn that bridge when we come to it," I said. "For now, you need to stay in charge. Surely there's some kind of provision for that."

Nathan piped up. "In the event of a candidate's death before they have signed the paperwork and been sworn in, the current mayor will serve on an interim basis until a new election can be scheduled within 180 days." It was almost as though he'd memorized the page where it had been recorded.

For all I knew, he had.

"As interim mayor then," George said with a shrug, "but as soon as possible, there's going to be another election. I'm not about to wait six months for a resolution to this mess."

"Do you honestly think that *anybody's* going to be brave enough to run against you after what happened to the last candidate?" Nathan asked. Was that an attempt at a joke? If so, it couldn't have come at a worse time.

George stood within two inches of his face. "Are you saying that you think *I* killed Lily Hamilton?"

"No, sir, of course not. I was just trying to ease the tension of the situation," Nathan explained as he involuntarily took a few steps back.

"Well, you failed at it miserably," George said.

"Come on, Nathan," the police chief said as he took the man's arm. "You can watch me pull these ballots out, and then we can go through them together in my office. I want to see if there's anything else of importance in there besides votes."

"I'm coming, too," George said.

"Of course, Mr. Mayor," Nathan said with obvious deference, no doubt trying to make up for his ill-timed attempt at humor. "It's only fitting."

"Then let's go," the police chief said. After he'd removed the ballots from the box and slid them into an oversized evidence bag, he handed it to Nathan and took the murder weapon himself. "I'm not leaving this in my trunk. I won't feel good about it until it's locked up in my office."

"I won't feel good about it even then," George said.

As they started to leave together, the chief stopped and looked at us. "What about you two? Do you want to tag along, too?"

"Thanks, but your office isn't big enough for all of us," Jake said.

I'd been about to eagerly accept the police chief's invitation, but after my husband had made that comment, all I could do was add, "Just let us know if you find anything out of the ordinary inside, would you?"

"This entire mess is out of the ordinary, but I'll be in touch," the chief said.

After they were gone, I turned to my husband. "I'm not second-guessing you, but *why* exactly did you turn the chief down just now?"

"Because we need to find out who wanted to get rid of Lily Hamilton ourselves, and we aren't going to be able to do that watching Nathan Billings count votes that ultimately don't matter one way or the other," Jake said.

"So, we're going to investigate this murder ourselves?" I asked.

"You don't object, do you?"

"No, sir," I said hastily. "I'm just surprised that *you're* so willing to jump in with both feet."

Jake frowned. "Think about it, Suzanne. Someone went to great lengths to make our friend look like a murderer, and in the process, they killed another human being. You heard Nathan. He claimed to be joking, but before sunup, half this town is going to believe that George literally wiped out his competition if we don't prove otherwise."

"I couldn't agree with you more," I said. "Where should we start?"

"That should be easy enough. Who was Lily's best friend?" he asked me.

"It might not be as easy as you think. If you ask me, it's got to be Gabby Williams."

"You're kidding, right?" Jake asked me. "I thought *you* were the only one in April Springs who could stand her."

"Keep your voice down," I warned my husband, though no one else was nearby at the moment. Gabby was barely viable as a friend, but as a sworn enemy, she would be hard to beat. "She and Lily go way back, so if anyone disliked Lily enough to kill her, Gabby would know."

"Then let's go talk to her," Jake said.

I hated to express what I had to say next, but I really had no choice. "Thanks for the offer, but I'm afraid that I need to talk to her alone. She won't open up in front of you. I'm really sorry."

Jake smiled as he touched my shoulder lightly. "Are you kidding? I was *hoping* you'd say that. Gabby and I try to tolerate each other, mostly because she's still not sure whether I'm good enough for you or not even now."

"She *can* be a bit overprotective of me," I admitted.

"That's putting it mildly."

"What are you going to do while I talk to Gabby?" I asked him.

"Oh, you know me. I'm going to snoop around a bit and see what the town gossip is saying. You've taught me never to ignore the human element in small towns, Suzanne."

"That's nice of you to say, but the things *you* have taught *me* are beyond measure," I said. I kissed my husband soundly, and then I went off in search of Gabby. If she wasn't home, I wasn't sure where I needed to look for her, but fortunately for me, she answered the door almost before my finger left the bell.

"Oh, it's you, Suzanne," Gabby said, clearly disappointed that I'd been the one who'd just shown up on her doorstep.

"I've had warmer greetings in my life, but I'll take what I can get," I said. "May I come in?"

She looked a bit annoyed with my request. "This isn't a good time."

"Then I'll be brief," I said as I walked right past her and into her living room.

"You've gotten a bit too familiar with me, young lady," Gabby announced, trying to make her voice sound as though it were full of doom.

"You know you love me," I said with a grin. "I'm here to talk about Lily Hamilton."

"She won, didn't she? As soon as she finishes up at the party, she's coming over here to give me a firsthand account of how it felt to beat George Morris."

"Are you telling me that you weren't at city hall earlier?" I asked, realizing that I hadn't seen her since the day before. "You don't know then, do you?"

"Know what?" she asked, clearly troubled by my question. "Don't tell me she actually lost! She'll be devastated." Gabby grabbed her jacket and headed for the front door. "I need to go comfort her, Suzanne. Step aside."

"Gabby, I'm afraid I've got some bad news, and it's worse than just the election results."

My friend looked as though she didn't believe it for one second. "What could possibly be worse than her losing to George?"

"I don't know how to tell you this, Gabby, but Lily's dead."

"Dead?" Gabby asked me incredulously. "What happened? Was it her heart?"

"No, I'm afraid someone hit her over the head with a ballot box," I said, having a difficult time believing what had happened myself, even though I'd seen the results of the murder with my own eyes.

"Suzanne, if you're trying to be funny, it's in very bad taste," Gabby said, and then she bit her lower lip.

"I wish I were, but I'm afraid she's really gone," I said, touching my friend's shoulder lightly and trying to offer her any bit of consolation that I could.

"But I just spoke with her a few hours ago," Gabby said as she fell back into a chair. "She was fine. Well, of course she was. That happened *before* someone killed her. Who did it, Suzanne? It wasn't George, was it?"

"Of course not," I said, quickly defending my friend. "George Morris would *never* do anything like that, and we both know it."

"I don't know what to think at the moment," Gabby said. "I can't believe she's gone."

"I'm so very sorry. Can you think of *anyone* who might want to see her dead?" I asked Gabby.

"Do you mean *besides* the mayor?"

"Gabby Williams, don't make me say it again. We *both* know that George Morris might not have liked the fact that Lily was running against him, but he would *never* have hurt her. Give me some names I can use."

"Does that mean that *you're* trying to solve her murder?" Gabby asked me.

"I am," I said. There was no sense denying it. Gabby knew about my proclivities to dig into murder on occasion.

She looked at me shrewdly for a full three seconds. "Tell me something, Suzanne. Are you doing it for Lily, or to clear George's name?"

"Why can't it be both?" I asked her. I wasn't about to lie to her. Our relationship was based on us telling each other the truth, no matter how painful it might be for the other person to hear, and I wouldn't have it any other way.

"It's simple. You have to be on Lily's side or George's," she said. "It can't be both."

"That's not true at all," I said, "but if you don't care enough about your late friend to help me solve her murder, then I don't know why I'm wasting valuable time talking to you when I could be out there tracking down her killer."

I started to leave, but Gabby reached out and grabbed my arm before I could go. What I'd just said wasn't a bluff, and she knew it. If I had to go right through my friend to get to the truth, then I'd steamroll over her without looking back, and what was more, she knew it.

"Hang on. I'll help you," she said softly.

I suddenly felt guilty for being so harsh with her, but sometimes—with some people—that was the only thing they responded to.

"Good," I said as I gently peeled her hand off my arm and sat back down. "I didn't know Lily nearly as well as I probably should have, so I'm going to have to rely on you to fill in some of the blanks. Besides you, who were her other friends? Did she have any enemies? In particular, is there anyone you know who might want to see her dead? I know I'm asking you a lot of questions at a time when you're trying to deal with your grief, but the faster we catch the killer, the better it will be for everyone involved, including Lily's memory."

Gabby nodded, lost in a fog. I thought for a moment that she'd forgotten that I was even there, but after nearly a minute, she finally spoke. "Everybody knows that Lily wasn't the most popular woman in April Springs. She wanted to be the president of every club she belonged to, and that ruffled quite a few feathers, especially over the last three or four weeks."

"Gabby, I'm talking about serious squabbles, not some inconsequential club politics."

"Then you've clearly not participated in many small groups if you believe that they don't matter to the people in them. The backstabbing and infighting can be enough to curl a seasoned politician's toes, things get so brutal and bloody sometimes."

"Enough to give someone a motive to commit murder?" I asked, incredulous at the very thought of the idea. I knew people got worked up sometimes in small groups, but to be angry enough to commit murder? It was hard for me to believe.

"Okay, maybe *all* of them might not be that desperate, but at least a few of them would be capable of killing to protect their status," Gabby said. "I hope you have a piece of paper and a pen."

"I'm ready if you are," I said as I pulled one of Jake's small notebooks out of my pocket as well as a pen. I'd been using the pad for a grocery list for the cottage, but this was much more important. After tearing off my partial list that included, "Eggs, Milk, Bread, Cheese," I wrote the name Lily Hamilton across the top. "Shoot," I said.

"I'm not even sure where to begin," she finally admitted.

"We can take it in any order that you'd like," I told her. "Just start talking, and I'll stop you when I have a question."

"Very well," Gabby said, and then she leaned back in her seat and started talking.

"The first name on your list should be Mercy Host. She's been complaining about Lily nonstop for the past few months. Lily beat her out of three different chair positions, and Mercy has said some pretty nasty things about her."

I wrote the name down. I knew Mercy slightly, but contrary to popular belief, not everyone in a small town knew each other. Momma probably knew her though, so I'd have to ask for an assessment of the woman's character. "Who else is on your list?"

"Jessie Carlton," she said.

After I wrote the woman's name down, I asked, "Why does she deserve to go on my list?"

"It's more of a feeling than an actual fact," Gabby said a bit uncertainly. "Jessie has pretended to be Lily's best friend for years, even practically running her campaign, but I've seen a few looks she's given Lily lately that make me wonder if she hasn't been simmering in the resentment of always being second fiddle to Lily. I'm sorry I can't give you more than that, but it's all I've got. Suzanne, you need to find out who did this to Lily, and make sure that they are punished for it."

"I'll do what I can, Gabby. Thanks for helping."

As I closed up my notebook, she said, "I can help you dig into this. I've got quite a few powerful friends in April Springs."

She also had more than her share of influential enemies, but I wasn't about to be the one who pointed that out to her. "If something comes up that suits your particular talents, I'll be sure to let you know."

"Do that," Gabby said.

I stood to go, but she didn't move.

"Gabby, are you okay?" I asked her softly as I hovered over her.

"The older I get, the more friends I seem to lose," she said in a tone of voice I was unfamiliar with, at least coming from her. This powerful and independent woman sounded beaten down to me, and it shook me more than I wanted to admit to hear it. "Suzanne, take care of yourself. I can't afford to lose you, too."

I touched her shoulder lightly. "I'll do my best. Is it okay if I take off now? I hate leaving you alone."

"I'll be fine," she said, suddenly seeming to pull herself together, or at least pretending to. "Now go. I have too many things to do to sit around here chatting with you and feeling sorry for myself."

"I'll show myself out then," I said, hiding my smile. She was putting on a brave front, and what was more, we both knew it.

As I left Gabby's place, I knew that I needed to speak with my husband as soon as possible before any of the details of what she'd just told me slipped my mind.

Chapter 4

AS I GOT BACK INTO my Jeep I pulled out my phone to call Jake when, much to my surprise, it rang in my hands before I could speed-dial him.

Even crazier was the fact that it was my husband calling me.

"I was just getting ready to call you," I started to say when he interrupted me.

"Suzanne, there's something I need to talk to you about, and it can't wait."

He was clearly unhappy about something. That much was obvious from his tone of voice and the way he'd cut me off before I could fill him in on what I'd just learned from Gabby.

"What happened? Did the chief already catch the killer?" I knew that it was possible, but I couldn't imagine it being all that likely. It wasn't that Stephen Grant wasn't a good cop, and getting better all the time, but that was asking a lot.

I thought this was going to be a harder case to solve.

"No. He admits that he's a bit in over his head. He and the mayor have gotten together, and they've conspired to draft me."

"You're not a pro ball player, Jake. What do you mean, draft you?"

"Sorry, that was a poor choice of words. Technically, the city of April Springs has hired me as a consultant to investigate the murder of Lily Hamilton. Since she's the mayor-elect, at least as far as Nathan Billings is concerned, it's town business, not that he approved of my hiring. In fact, he fought it a bit before he finally gave in."

"Why would he do that?" I asked him. "You're more than qualified for the job."

"He seems to be under the distinct impression that until he determines who *really* won the election, nobody else should do anything about the investigation."

"I didn't think he was going to allow those ballots to be counted," I said.

"He's had a change of heart. Evidently we're still going to have a special election, but at the moment, he's not even willing to certify that George can remain mayor until we can have it."

"Does he really have that much influence over it?"

"You know how it is. With some folks, the less power they have, the more they try to use it."

"Funny, but Gabby just said the very same thing to me. In fact..."

He interrupted me again. "I'm sorry, but I really can't talk right now. They're waiting on me in George's office, at least what is his office for now. We'll catch up later tonight, okay? I just wanted you to know that I can't investigate this case with you. Are you okay with that?"

"It's fine, Jake. After all, George needs us in any way that we can help. I'll find someone else," I said. It was hard to hide my disappointment, and I knew that it wasn't really the answer he'd been hoping for, but there wasn't much I could do about it.

"Suzanne, I honestly didn't have much choice," he replied, and I could hear the angst in his voice about accepting the job without talking to me about it first.

"Jake, it's okay. Really," I said. "As long as we are both working to clear George's name, as far as I'm concerned, we're on the same team."

"You're really going to keep digging into this yourself then?" he asked.

"Is there any doubt in your mind?" I countered.

"No. Just get Grace to help you. Do that much for me."

"I'll go see her right now and ask her," I said. "You did the right thing accepting their offer, Jake."

"Thanks for understanding. They backed me into a corner, and I couldn't seem to be able to say no."

"I get that completely. Go get 'em, tiger," I said, and added a slight chuckle to it.

"You're the best, Suzanne."

"Right back at you," I answered.

In the background, I could hear Chief Grant as he said, "Jake, we need you in this meeting right now."

"Sorry, but I've gotta run," Jake told me, and then he hung up.

It was at that point that I realized that I hadn't even shared the two names Gabby had given me to investigate.

Well, at least I'd tried.

As I drove over to Grace's house, I hoped that she'd be free to help me. If she wasn't, I could always ask Momma, or even Phillip, but my best friend was my next best choice, especially if my husband wasn't available. The dynamic with Grace and the one with Jake were totally different, though they were equally effective.

Both were good, just not in the same way, but I needed a partner for this investigation, and I hoped that Grace could do it.

"Suzanne, I'm really sorry, but my new boss is making me account for every minute of my day that I'm supposed to be working. Can you imagine that?"

Grace was truly appalled by this new development, and it took all I had not to giggle. After all, didn't *most* bosses expect that of their employees? I'd worked for myself for so long that it was hard for me to remember sometimes. "Who would have thought that was possible?" I asked her.

"I know, right?" She studied my face for a moment. "Hang on. Are you teasing me?"

"Grace, you have to admit that you've had it easy for the past few years. Your supervisors have pretty much left you alone to do whatever you wanted to."

"I guess," she admitted reluctantly. "This one's trying to make a name for herself with the new company that bought us. She's going to claw her way to the top no matter how many bodies she has to climb on to get there."

"That's good though, right?" I asked her.

"In what universe is that a *good* thing?" she asked me incredulously.

"Think about it. She won't be around long if she's on her way up, and if she makes too many people upset with her micromanaging style, she won't last long as a supervisor. Either way, chances are pretty good that you won't have to deal with her this time next year."

"An entire year of that woman?" she asked in disbelief. "I don't know if I'll last a month, let alone a year."

"You can do it," I said. "I have faith in you."

"I'm glad one of us does," she said with a grin, stealing one of my own usual replies.

"Do you have any advice for me?" she asked.

"If I were in your shoes, I'd give her *more* than she's asking for."

"What do you mean?"

"Grace, if she wants to know what you're doing every minute of the day, I'd make sure to tell her, literally. Report the most insignificant thing you do as the greatest achievement. Overblow everything and inundate her with emails, texts, and phone calls. Make her get to the point where she longs for the days when you weren't under her direct supervision."

Grace seemed to consider that for a moment before she spoke again. "Isn't that going to make me look unprofessional?"

"Do you have the latest email she sent you telling you to report what you're doing to her?" I asked.

"Sure, it's still on my phone." She brought up the email and read it to me. "'Grace, I need to know where you are and what you're doing every minute of the workday. Things are going to change around here or else.' Charming, isn't she?"

"If she wants you to follow her orders, I'd do it literally if I were you. You have her email to back up your position, and if she protests that it's too much, then you can pull back and let her think that she won."

"It might just work," Grace said. "How did you come up with it?"

"Remember Mrs. Hardesty in the eleventh grade? She demanded complete accountability about our status on our science reports, so we flooded her with updates to the point where *she* started ducking *us* in the hallway."

"I remember," Grace said with a smile. "I don't know. It might just work. Suzanne, you're brilliant."

"Don't give me the credit. If you recall, it was your idea back then, and I don't see any reason it won't work now," I told her.

"It's got to at least be worth a shot. In the meantime, I hate to do it, but I'm going to have to say no to investigating Lily Hamilton's murder with you. Can you get someone else to help?"

"I'm sure of it," I said. "Don't worry about me."

"I do though, you know," she answered soberly. "I'll tell you what. If you can't find anyone else, I'll do it."

"What about your job?" I asked her seriously.

"Suzanne, I can *always* get another job. Best friends, on the other hand, are a bit harder to replace. I mean it. Call me, and I'll come running."

"I appreciate the thought, but I'm sure that it won't come to that."

She wouldn't let it go, though. "With Jake and me out of the picture, who's next on your list? It can't be George. He's in this too deep already."

"I wasn't going to ask him," I told her. "I was thinking about Momma, and if she can't do it, then Phillip."

"It's funny, isn't it?" Grace asked with a smile.

"What's that?"

"When you investigated your first murder, Chief Martin was the last person on earth you'd ever ask for help."

"It's true, but a lot has changed since then," I reminded her.

"Well, he's your stepfather now," she said with a shrug.

"There's more to it than that. I actually like the man. He's got more good points than I ever imagined back in the day. My question is did *he* change, or did *I*?"

"Truth be told, I think it's probably a little bit of both," she said. She was about to add something else when her phone rang. "That's Linda the Hun. I'd better take it."

"Good luck," I said as I left her.

Grace would be fine. There was no doubt about it in my mind. She'd weather this storm just as she had all the ones that had come before it and would go on after her current supervisor was nothing but a distant memory.

In the meantime, I had to find a partner to investigate this crime, and I had to do it quickly.

"I see Momma's car is gone. Do you know when she'll be back?" I asked my stepfather when he answered the door to the cottage they shared. The former chief of police's waistline had definitely shrunk some as of late, and I knew that he'd been working diligently to recapture some of his old form. "Exactly how much weight have you lost, Phillip?"

"Seventeen pounds," he said proudly. "The older I get, the harder it seems to be to lose it. Once I hit my target goal again, I'm going to stay on the straight and narrow."

"Does that mean that you're swearing off donuts for good?" I asked him. I knew the man enjoyed my treats, and he also hated to disappoint me, so it hadn't really been a fair question.

"No, I'm trying to live like this for the rest of my life, and if I thought I had to go without ever tasting your donuts again, I'm not sure I'd have the will to go on." He said it with a grin, and I smiled back at him.

"Maybe *you* should run for mayor if George really walks away," I told him. "That was a pretty slick answer you just gave me."

"No thanks," he said, his smile vanishing. "I don't need the headaches. In fact, I'm not quite sure why George is so gung-ho about keeping the job, especially after what happened to Lily Hamilton. Are you and Jake looking into Lily's murder?"

I knew better than to deny it. "I am, at least. George and Chief Grant have hired my husband as a consultant on the case."

"That's a smart move," the former chief said. "So then it's you and Grace."

"She can't do it because she has some work issues," I admitted.

"Well, I know you're not here for *me* as a partner. Your mother just ran out to the store. She should be back any second."

"Actually, I was hoping to recruit *both* of you," I said, making it up on the spot as I went along.

"You want me as well?" he asked, clearly surprised.

"Why not? We've worked together successfully before," I said, remembering a few cases where his assistance had definitely been a help to my investigations. He had been a decent cop, though I hadn't realized it at the time, and his work with long-dead cold cases had just improved his skill set as far as I was concerned.

"I'm flattered, Suzanne," he said.

"Even though you and Momma weren't at the top of my list?" I asked him.

"Hey, it's fine company you keep, so there aren't any slights as far as I'm concerned."

"So, what do you say?" I asked, warming up to the idea more and more as I considered the possibilities. Phillip had connections in law enforcement, while Momma knew the social scene inside and out, even if she chose to stay on the perimeter of it.

"Well, I can't speak for your mother, but if you want me, I'm in," he said with a smile.

"Excellent," I said as Momma walked in behind me.

"What's excellent?" she asked me as her husband took one of the grocery bags from her.

"Suzanne's recruiting us to help solve Lily Hamilton's murder," Phillip said with a smile.

"*Both* of us?" she asked much as her husband had earlier.

"That's what I asked her," Phillip replied.

"Okay, I admit that Jake and Grace were both busy, but I think we're the best team there is to solve this murder. Between the three of us, we've got *all* the bases covered."

"I don't know," Momma said reluctantly as she walked into the kitchen, with us following her. As she started putting groceries away, she added, "Suzanne, we really shouldn't meddle."

"We won't be directly interfering with the police investigation," I said, trying to reassure her. "We'll stay out on the edges. Jake and Chief Grant can work the heart of the case. We'll just dig around in the areas they don't think to cover."

"What's Jake got to do with the official investigation?" Momma asked as she continued to put things away.

"Chief Grant and the mayor hired him as a consultant," Phillip supplied.

"And Grace? Why can't she help you?" Momma asked.

"She's dealing with some work issues," I said, not really wanting to get into it with them.

"Come on, Dot. It could be fun," Phillip told his wife gently.

"Digging into murder isn't now, nor has it ever been, my idea of fun," she replied.

"Okay, how about this, then? Phillip and I will take the lead in the investigation, and you can act as a consultant for us. There are some ins and outs of the local club scene that we're going to need you for, but otherwise, we'll keep you out of the direct line of snooping. Surely you can do that much."

"Yes, I'd be comfortable with that role," she said. "Phillip? Is that acceptable to you?"

"Hey, I've told you all along, my dear. I'll take you however I can get you."

She leaned forward and kissed him, and I didn't feel the urge to turn away. That was progress, especially when I remembered how I'd acted when they'd first gotten together. Maybe it was true that we were all growing, at least a little.

"Then it's settled," Momma said. "Why don't you two get together and discuss the case while I make us all a late snack."

I glanced at the clock and realized that it was already past my bedtime. I was scheduled to make donuts in the morning, and it was too late to ask Emma and Sharon to take over for me. Honestly, I didn't like doing that unless it couldn't be helped. I *enjoyed* making the treats I sold to the kind folks of April Springs, and besides, sometimes I got unexpected information working the counter right after a murder.

"Can I take a rain check?" I asked her.

"Of course," she said.

I turned to Phillip. "How about if we get started tomorrow after I close Donut Hearts for the day?"

"I guess that would be okay," my stepfather said a bit reluctantly.

"I'm serious, Phillip. We do this together, or we don't do it at all. I don't want to find out that you've been digging into this case without me. Are we clear?"

He saluted me. "Yes, ma'am. You're in charge. I'm just your sidekick." He added a grin to the last part.

Momma gave him a quick kiss. "I think you're a *fine* sidekick," she said with a smile of her own. "Suzanne, he'll behave himself. I promise."

"Should you really be making promises for your husband?" I asked her, only half joking.

"About this? Absolutely," she said. "Now off you go back home. Phillip will see you at the shop at eleven sharp tomorrow morning."

"Well, I still have a few chores to do once I lock the front door," I reminded her.

"Hey, a broom handle fits my hand just as well as it does yours," he said. "I'll see you then."

"Bye," I replied as I headed for the door.

"Suzanne, thanks for including me," Phillip said before I could go.

"Are you kidding? I'm the one who should be thanking you," I told him. "You're really helping me out here."

He nodded, and the smile I saw on his face had been worth me asking him for his help.

I had been gone less than three minutes when my phone rang. To my surprise, it was Momma.

I pulled over and answered her call. "Hey. Long time no see. What happened, did I forget my jacket there or something?" I asked her.

"No, at least I don't think so. I just wanted to thank you for asking Phillip to help you on the case. He gets restless sometimes, and this will be good for him. Just don't go getting him killed, will you? I've gotten used to having him around." She was clearly joking about it, but I knew how much she was concerned about his well-being, especially after he'd gone through his bout with cancer. Life was more precious to them now, and I didn't want to do anything to take that away.

"I'll do my best, but I can't make any promises," I said. With a chuckle, I added, "I've gotten used to him, too. I'll take care of him, Momma."

"I know you will, sweet girl," my mother answered.

"You've already had the same conversation with Phillip about him looking out for me, haven't you?" I asked, not really guessing at all.

"I refuse to answer on the grounds that I might incriminate myself," she said with a smile in her voice.

"Good night, Momma. I love you bunches."

"And I love you twice as much," she said, and then we ended the call.

I knew she'd been partially joking about me looking out for her husband, but I was taking my promise to her seriously. If there was any way I could keep him out of danger, I'd do it. She'd given me so much in my life, I at least owed her that much.

Chapter 5

I'D BEEN HOPING TO see my husband when I got back to the cottage we shared on the edge of the park, but the moment I saw that his new-to-him old truck was gone, I knew that wasn't going to happen. Instead, I found a note from him.

Suzanne,

Sorry I missed you, but we're having a late night digging into this. Heard about Grace and her new boss from the chief, so I suspect you and your mother are digging into this together. I don't envy whoever did it if they have to face the two of you! Be careful. I hope one of us figures this out soon so our lives can get back to normal, whatever normal is for the two of us.

Love,

Jake.

I didn't even think about throwing the note away. Taking out my keepsake box from the closet Jake had built under the stairway, I carefully folded the note and added it to the stack of other ones he'd left me since we'd been together. Most of the people who knew me didn't think of me as being overly sentimental, and I wasn't even sure that Jake realized that I kept every note he'd ever written me, but I was extremely syrupy when it came to my husband.

I grabbed a quick bite from the fridge and then headed off to bed. Granted, I would have rather been with him, but knowing how much he loved me was enough to help me sleep peacefully. When I woke up at 2:45 the next morning, he was snoring softly beside me. I thought about waking him, but the poor man sounded exhausted, so I dressed quietly, as was my custom, and then I made my way into the kitchen. There I had a quick bowl of cereal and was ready to leave when I decided to leave him a note of my own. I doubted Jake treasured mine the way I did the ones I got from him, but I wanted him to know that I was thinking of him, too.

Jake my love,

You were sleeping so peacefully I didn't have the heart to wake you. Crimefighting is exhausting business, isn't it? Phillip is helping me out, and Momma is acting as our consultant, so I'm in good hands, though not as good as when I'm in yours. Never fear, I'm certain one of us will find Lily's killer soon enough, and we will indeed get back to our own, wonderful version of normal.

In the meantime, watch your back, as I promise to watch mine!

Love in Bunches and Bunches,

Suzanne.

I folded it in half and propped it up on the counter where I was sure he'd see it, and then I left the cottage to make my three-minute commute to Donut Hearts. I had a lot to think about while I made the cake donuts first and then the yeast ones. There wasn't going to be a great deal of time to get lost in the donutmaking process, since this was the one day of the week that I made donuts by myself. This morning, I'd have my hands full, or at least my thoughts, with strategies to find Lily Hamilton's killer as I created my tasty masterpieces for the public.

At least that was my plan.

Who knew how it would work out in the end? My days, even the most mundane ones, rarely played out the way I imagined they would, especially when there was an ongoing murder investigation.

As I parked in front of Donut Hearts, the streetlight behind me went out. In fact, every light I could see went dark all at once. I walked to the door of the donut shop, found the key slot mostly by memory, and then walked into the shop and flipped on the light.

Or tried to, at any rate.

It was pitch dark inside there as well.

Remembering my phone had a flashlight app on it, I pulled it out and used the bright light to let myself out. I was standing outside of the shop, wondering what to do next and who I should call about the outage, when a power company truck pulled up.

"My lights are out," I said.

"The whole block is out, ma'am," the young man said. "We're working on a transformer near city hall, but I'm afraid we're not going to have your power restored for at least an hour."

I tried to think how that would work for me. I could either make the yeast donuts given the time I had, or do the cake donuts, but I knew that I didn't have time to do both. Which should I do, though? Clearly I had time to think about it. After all, I had at least an hour before I could do anything at all. "Thanks for coming by and telling me."

"You didn't get a chance to make coffee or donuts before the power went out, did you?" he asked me. "My boss sent me over here to check."

"Sorry, but I just got here myself," I said. "Tell you what. If you'll give me an hour after you get my power going again, I'll treat you all to both."

"As much as we'd appreciate that, I'm sure we'll have to take a rain check. We've got old transformers all around this part of the state, and for some reason, they're going out without any rhyme or reason. We could be in Union Square or Maple Hollow by the time you have donuts ready."

"Well, if you're still in town, the offer stands," I said. "You say I've got an hour?"

"If I were to guess, I'd say that it will most likely be more like two or three," he admitted. "We've got to wait for the new transformers to be delivered from Charlotte, and the truck hasn't even left the depot yet."

That made my decision easier. It would be cake donuts today or nothing, since I wouldn't have time to make the yeast variety. My customers would just have to live with it. After all, some donuts had to be better than no donuts at all. "I'll be back in a few hours, then."

After he was gone, I got into my Jeep and headed back to the cottage. There was no sense hanging around in the dark, waiting to get my power back. I set my battery-powered alarm once I got back home, and then I slipped back into bed beside Jake.

"What's going on? What happened? Shouldn't you be making donuts?" he asked groggily.

"There was a power outage. Go back to sleep," I said.

"'kay. Love you."

"I love you, too," I said, but I could swear that he was already asleep again by the time I told him. Jake could usually drop off given the slightest opportunity, something I envied greatly in him. It took me all of three minutes to get back to sleep myself.

Two minutes before my alarm was set to go off, I woke up on my own. My internal alarm clock was usually pretty good. I suspected it came from years of working at Donut Hearts, knowing exactly when to flip the donuts and then pull them out, all based on feel and not a clock. That didn't mean that I didn't still set my alarms though, including the one I used during my morning breaks with Emma. After all, it was a nice skill to have, but I wasn't willing to rely on it a hundred percent.

I glanced up to see our plug-in alarm clock flashing, and it only showed 12:07, so the power had come back on only seven minutes ago. The extra sleep had been worth losing a handful of minutes of baking time, but I hurriedly got dressed and headed back to the shop.

The streetlights greeted me as I hit the main section of Springs Drive, and I saw that I'd left the front light of Donut Hearts on when I'd taken off earlier. At least it made it easy enough to see the door-lock this time.

Hurrying inside, I got busy the second I made it inside, flipping on the fryer and the coffee pot and then getting my kitchen ready for a shortened day. I had only an hour before it was time to open my doors, and I knew that I'd better get busy.

Promptly at six a.m., I opened the front door to find the mayor—I refused to call him anything else—waiting for me.

"I wasn't sure you'd be open at all today after the power outage," George Morris said as I stepped aside to let him in.

"I didn't have time to make raised donuts, but I've got eight kinds of cake donuts if you're interested," I said. I'd made extra to compensate for the lack of yeast donuts on the menu for the morning, and the cases were full, albeit lacking one of my main staples.

"I'll take a coffee, an apple-filled donut, and hey, a pumpkin one, too," he said. "I'm surprised to see that back on the menu this time of year."

"Desperate times call for desperate measures," I said as I put his order together. "Is this to go, or will you be eating here?"

"I'm not in any hurry to get to the office," he admitted. "Do you mind if I hang out here with you for a while?"

"George, you know you're *always* welcome at my counter," I told him affectionately. "How are you holding up?"

"I didn't sleep much last night, if that's what you're asking. I don't particularly like being the lead suspect in a murder investigation."

"I understand that feeling all too well," I told him. I'd been in that position myself in the past, and I knew from personal experience that it wasn't a pleasant experience, to say the least. "Don't worry. You've got friends digging into this to find out the truth."

"I know. I'm glad Jake was free to join Chief Grant on this," he admitted as he took a bite of pumpkin. "Wow, I forgot just how good these things are. Why don't you box up half a dozen for me before they're all gone?"

"I can do that," I said. I'd suspected that I'd have a run on those particular treats, since they were one of my most popular donuts in the cool weather. It was warm outside now, but I'd had a hunch that I'd have no trouble moving them, so I'd made a double batch of pumpkin just in case. Worst-case scenario if I was wrong, I'd have a lot of goodies to give away at the end of the day, and today I could live with that. Besides, if Phillip and I had as busy an afternoon ahead of us as I thought, it wouldn't hurt having three or four dozen extra donuts with us to encourage folks to talk to us. It was amazing what a free donut or two could do to loosen someone's lips. "They aren't the only ones digging into this," I reminded me.

"I heard. Jake told me last night that you and Chief Martin were going to help out, too."

"Unofficially, of course," I said.

"Suzanne, as far as I'm concerned, they should put you on the payroll. You do as much detecting as *whoever* our chief of police happens to be," he said as he took a sip of coffee.

"No, thanks," I said. "If I agreed to that, then *I'd* have to follow the rules."

"And we can't have that, can we?" he asked with a slight grin. "What's on your plate today?"

"Do you mean besides selling donuts?" I asked him.

"Of course. I know that's your first priority."

"Don't be so sure," I said. "My friends are more important than my business is to me," I added as I reached over and patted his hand.

"You're just what I needed this morning," he said with a gentle smile. "You and your goodies," he added.

I was about to respond when the front door opened again.

It was Ray Blake this time, and he was heading straight for the mayor.

"Mayor, would you care to comment on the death of the *real* mayor of April Springs?" Ray asked as he stood near George.

Ignoring the newspaperman completely, George looked at me with pressed lips. "I'll take this to go after all, Suzanne."

As I hurriedly bagged his remaining treats and grabbed a to-go cup for his coffee, Ray pushed him further. "Don't the voters have a right to know?"

"No comment," George said as he stood. Pulling a ten-dollar bill from his wallet, he slid it across the counter toward me.

"Let me get your change," I said.

"Use it to buy the next customer a donut or two," he said. "Except for him," he added as he gestured back toward the newspaperman. "He can buy his own donuts."

"Hey, I heard that," Ray protested.

"Good. You were meant to," George said as he started to go.

Ray Blake foolishly stood his ground.

Were we going to have trouble in the donut shop? Surely the newspaperman knew better than to try to block George from leaving.

The mayor stopped and stared at Ray Blake for five seconds before speaking. "Move."

It wasn't said violently, or even with the hint of a threat, but it was enough. George's meaning was clear. Move or be moved.

The newspaperman stepped to one side, and the mayor left.

"Ray, what have I told you about coming in here and causing trouble?" I asked him.

"Suzanne, he can't just ignore me. The people of April Springs deserve answers, and I aim to get them."

"You know my policy," I said as I pointed to the front door. "You have to leave."

"I know," he said a bit glumly, and then he glanced over at the display cases. "Are those pumpkin donuts?"

"They are, but you can't have any," I said.

"You can't refuse to sell me donuts just because you don't like the way I conduct my business," he protested.

I pointed to the sign above the register that said I had the right to refuse service to anyone I pleased. "That says differently," I told him.

"Come on, Suzanne. Just one," he pled.

I didn't want to do it, but then again, I couldn't afford to have Emma or Sharon mad at me, either. Without them, I'd be working Donut Hearts seven days a week all alone, and that was something I was not prepared to do.

"Fine. You can have one donut, but it's going to cost you double the regular price," I said.

"That's hardly fair," he protested.

"I could have said triple. In fact, that's what I meant," I answered. "You're paying a jerk tax, Ray. You broke the rules. There are consequences to your actions."

"Okay, I get it," he said as he got out his wallet and slid a five across the counter. "Add my change to the mayor's. He's not the only one who can be generous."

"I can do that," I said. "For the extra money, I'll even throw in a napkin and a bag."

"Any chance I could get some coffee, too?" he asked hopefully.

"Don't get greedy," I said. "After all, you're still in my doghouse." I added the last bit with the hint of a smile. The truth was that I couldn't blame a snake for biting. That was what they did.

"Understood," he said as he took the bag, opened it slightly, and inhaled. "Man, that smells amazing."

"Thanks," I said. "Now, isn't there someplace else you need to be?"

"Gotcha," he said, and then he left the shop.

It hadn't been the best start to a day at Donut Hearts, but it hadn't been the worst one, either. I had a hunch that things were going to be rocky for a while, especially if we all had trouble figuring out who had killed Lily Hamilton. Life would be tense with the mayor under the entire town's scrutiny, and I had a feeling that the longer it went on, the worse things would get.

If Jake and Chief Grant didn't find the murderer, then at least I hoped that my stepfather and I could.

The fact of the matter was that I didn't care who did it, just that someone did.

The way I saw it, that was the *only* way that life in April Springs could get back to normal.

Chapter 6

"HEY, YOU'RE NEVER HERE at this time of day. What's going on?" I asked Paige Hall a few minutes before ten. "Shouldn't you be opening the bookstore about now?"

"I should be, but I figured they could wait for me for a change. I'll have two apple fritters and a coffee to go, please." As I made her change and got her order together, Paige studied me a moment before asking, "What's going on with the investigation?"

"How should I know?" I asked loftily. Did Paige already know that Phillip and I were digging into the mayor-elect's murder? If so, word was spreading particularly fast, even for April Springs.

"I thought Jake was working with the police," she said with a frown.

"Oh, that. Yes, he is."

"What am I missing here, Suzanne?" Paige was one of the smartest people in April Springs, at least as far as I was concerned. Not two seconds later, she said, "You're investigating her murder too, aren't you? I heard that Grace was tied up with business, and if Jake's working with the police, that leaves the mayor, your mother, or your stepfather as potential partners in crime. If I had to guess, the mayor offered to help, but you had to decline, since he's got to be the main suspect in the case. So which is it, Phillip or your mother?"

"Phillip," I admitted, since no one else was in Donut Hearts at the moment. "That's some first-class deduction, lady. Maybe I should have asked you to help me instead."

She laughed. "No, thank you. If it's all the same to you, I'll keep my sleuthing to the books I read and sell," she replied. "It's so much cleaner and neater that way."

"Just out of curiosity, how do you know so much about my sideline?" I asked.

"Is that what you're calling your murder investigations these days? Do you want to know how I know what goes on around here? I listen, mainly," she said. "That and the fact that I've read more cozy mysteries than just about anyone else alive. If you read enough of them, you start to see intrigue everywhere you look. Plus, I know for a fact that you like to get involved, but only when folks you care about are in a mess that's usually up to their eyebrows. Now that I think about it, I've got some information that you might be able to use."

"That would be great. I'm all ears," I said.

"I hope not. What a horrible thought," she answered with a groan. "Anyway, I saw Mercy Host looking for something behind my shop when I got in this morning. The police must have just cleared the area where you found Lily's body, and it was way too early for me to be in the store, but I got a new shipment of books in last night, and I wanted to get them on the shelves this morning."

"I wonder what she was looking for?" I asked.

"I have no idea, but it couldn't have been all that big, since she was down on her hands and knees, combing through the grass. Anyway, I thought I should tell someone."

"Do I count as someone in that scenario?" I asked her with a grin.

"You do in my book. Pass it on to Jake if you get the chance, would you?" Paige glanced over her shoulder at the bookstore, which was easy to see through my front window. "I'd better get going. It appears my readers are getting restless."

"That must be nice," I said.

"I don't know why you say that. You have more fans than I do," she said.

"I feed the body, but you feed the spirit and the mind," I corrected her.

"On my best day, maybe," she said. "Anyway, good luck."

"Thanks. I'm afraid I'm going to need it this time."

"If there's anything I can do to help the cause, you know where to find me," she said as she pointed to her bookshop across the street from Donut Hearts. "You know me. I'm usually there."

"Thanks, Paige," I said.

"You bet."

Ten minutes later, Gabby Williams walked into Donut Hearts.

"Hey, Gabby. Did you come by for a midmorning snack?" I asked her with a grin. "Or did you just miss me?"

"Suzanne, you aren't nearly as amusing as you think you are," Gabby said.

"Then what will you have?"

"I need to discuss something with you," she said in a serious manner.

"That sounds too much like 'we need to talk,' Gabby. What's going on? You're not leaving town again, are you?"

"No, just the opposite, in fact," Gabby replied. "I'm going to rebuild ReNEWed."

"That's wonderful news," I said as I walked around the counter and hugged her. She stiffened a bit at first, but just before she pushed away from me, I swore that I could feel her give in to my embrace for just a moment. For us, that was real progress.

"I'm not sure you're going to feel that way after I tell you the rest of it. We're breaking ground on the building next week, and I'm afraid you're going to be living in a construction zone for the next eight or nine months. I'm sorry, but there's nothing I can do about it."

She was clearly expecting me to complain, and while I wouldn't love the noise and disruption of the building process, it would be great having Gabby back next door again. I couldn't let her know that, though. She'd clearly been anticipating an argument, and it would disappoint her if I just folded.

"Gabby, that's terrible. They'll take up my customers' parking spots and leave mud everywhere. What happened to the idea of you just using another building?"

Was that a smile I saw cross her face? I couldn't tell. It had come and gone so quickly that I might have even imagined it. "Suzanne Hart, it's going to happen, so there's no use complaining about it. You're just going to have to live with the chaos until they can finish."

"Fine," I grumbled, though it was taking all of my acting ability not to look happy. Having a little chaos was a small price to pay to get Gabby back, but I couldn't let her see that. "If there's nothing I can do about it, then that's that."

"Have you made any progress figuring out what happened to Lily?" she asked, softening a bit.

"All I can report is that Phillip and I are digging into it," I told her. "Have you thought of anything else since we spoke yesterday?"

"Maybe one thing," Gabby said. "I'm not sure if it's relevant or not, though."

"Why don't you tell me and let me decide," I told her.

"I remembered something Lily told me the day before she died. She said that someone was trying to get her to quit the race, but she wasn't going to back down. Evidently they were rather melodramatic about it."

"Really? It wasn't George, was it?" I asked, dreading to hear her answer. That was all I needed was for the mayor to be implicated in trying to run his opponent out of the race before she was murdered. It could be argued that when his demand that she quit didn't work, he took matters into his own hands and eliminated his competition in a much harsher, and more final, way.

"No, of course not. The mayor and I have had our differences over the years, but I've come to think about what you said about him earlier, and I agree. He's an honorable man, and he wouldn't stoop to murder. I wouldn't put him past punching a man in the nose, but never a woman, let alone club her to death with a ballot box."

"I'm so glad that you feel that way," I said. "If it wasn't George, then who was it?"

"I'm not sure. All I can say with any certainty is that it was someone with their own agenda. If I were to guess, I'd say that it was someone active in the April Springs business scene, but that bit is pure conjecture on my part."

"Are you talking about Momma?" I asked, mortified. She'd never demand that Lily quit the race.

Would she?

"No, it wasn't Dorothea. I'm sure of that as well," Gabby said with disapproval. "Honestly, Suzanne, you should have more faith in the people who are closest to you."

"I do," I said, relieved that Gabby wasn't implicating either my mother or the current mayor. "But I still don't know who you're talking about."

"I don't either," she said. "If I were you, I'd follow the money, though."

"What do you mean by that?"

"It's just common sense, isn't it? I've been thinking about it ever since you told me what happened, and I keep coming back to one question. Who had the most to lose by Lily winning the election?"

"You mean besides George," I reminded her.

"I mean financially. If you'll remember, George's predecessor was into some dirty deeds before he was killed."

I remembered well enough, since I'd played a part in capturing the mayor's killer. "Does it always come down to money?"

"No, but you know as well as I do that greed is a powerful motive," Gabby said. "Anyway, I'm not here to talk about what happened to Lily. I just wanted to let you know that construction on my new shop will be starting within the next few weeks, no matter how unpleasant it is going to be for you and your business. That is if the permits are ever issued. Going through City Hall these days is like climbing uphill through a mudhole."

I didn't want to point out that I'd never seen a mudhole that you had to scale. Gabby had a point. I knew that permits and processes could take time, but at least she was staying in April Springs. I fully realized that I'd probably regret her presence again with her shop beside mine, but I also knew that my life was poorer without her in it, not that I'd ever tell her that. "You'll manage, I'm sure."

"I'm sure of it," she said. "Now I've got to be off."

"Would you like a donut for the road?" I offered. "It's on the house."

"No, I'd better not. I have enough bad habits as it is, so I don't need to cultivate any new ones at my age."

"Fair enough," I said.

"Suzanne Hart, was that a smile I just saw on your lips?"

"Me? No, ma'am. It must be a touch of indigestion. I had a bad bowl of cereal this morning."

Gabby looked as though she wanted to question how anyone could have a bad bowl of cereal, but apparently she thought better of it. "Very well. Remember, you've been warned."

"I have indeed," I said solemnly, doing my best to fight a smile. It appeared that Gabby was moving full steam ahead on her rebuilding.

That was fine by me.

But who could have threatened the mayor elect and tried to run her out of office? I'd have to keep my eyes open and maybe ask Momma as well. After all, if there *was* something going on in the business world that swirled around our town, if my mother wasn't a part of it, she'd know what was going on at the very least.

At least that was what I hoped.

"Hey, guys. What brings you by Donut Hearts? Isn't this a school day?"

Terri Milner and her twin girls came into the shop together. I hadn't seen them in weeks. I was suddenly concerned about them when I realized that the twins had recently been crying, though the tears had been wiped away, at least for the moment.

"We're playing hooky," Terri said softly.

"Really? You're the coolest mom ever," I said.

"Hang on a second," she told me, and then she turned to her daughters, who had to be at least ten or eleven by now, though I was terrible with kids' ages. "What can I get you ladies?"

"I want a double chocolate iced donut," Jerri said. "Momma, can I have two?" she asked her mother, who surprised me by nodding.

"Two it is," Terri said. "How about you, Mary?"

"I don't want anything," the young girl said sullenly.

"Come on, don't be that way," Jerri told her sister. "Order *something*."

"I don't want to," Mary insisted.

"Get *something*," Jerri insisted.

"Jerri, if your sister doesn't want a donut, she doesn't have to have one," Terri said firmly.

"I'll have a plain one, I guess," Mary finally conceded.

"Chocolate milk?" Terri asked her.

"Sure. I guess." She found a table as far away from the counter as she could, which wasn't saying all that much in my small shop. Jerri walked behind her, and I saw the two of them conferring in low whispers, Jerri clearly doing her best to comfort her twin.

"What's going on?" I asked Terri as I got the donut orders ready.

"Their aunt died yesterday," she said softly.

"Lily Hamilton was your sister?" I asked. I couldn't imagine that to be true even as I said it.

"What? No, Harry's sister was in a car accident outside of Chicago. We just found out, and Harry insisted that we tell the girls immediately. I thought it should wait until after school, but he was adamant."

"Where is he, by the way?" I asked as I grabbed a pair of milks.

"He's on the phone out in the car. Their folks have been gone for ages, so Harry is all that Cary had left as far as family or friends. It's all kind of sad, really."

"He didn't marry you because your name ends in 'I', did he?" I asked her softly, trying to ease a bit of her troubled spirit.

"I won't say that it didn't hurt," Terri answered. "Anyway, he's flying to Chicago to handle the arrangements, and he wanted to spend a little time with the girls before he had to leave for the airport in Asheville."

"You're not all going?" I asked her.

"I offered, but Harry wants to do this alone. He and Cary weren't all that close. She only came to April Springs once since the girls were born, but she always sent them checks for birthdays and Christmases."

"They seem to be taking it differently," I said, gesturing to the girls, who were still in conference in the corner.

"Jerri feels the loss too, but Mary has always been the one who shows her emotions more. It's amazing how twins can be so different sometimes."

Harry came in, nodded to us, and then headed straight for his daughters.

I added a few extra donuts and two coffees to the tray.

"Thanks," Terri said. "What do I owe you?"

"We're good," I said.

"I insist," she said firmly as she slipped a ten-dollar bill across the counter.

I knew better than to push it. "Thanks. If there's anything I can do like babysitting the girls, let me know," I answered.

"I appreciate that," she said, offering me the briefest of smiles as she took the tray and joined her family.

After they were gone ten minutes later, I cleaned up after them and took a moment to realize that the world was not just April Springs and that other people lived and died in it every day. It was a bit of a harsh reminder that none of us knew when our time was up, so it was important to make the most of it while we could. I felt sorry for Cary, not just for dying alone but for losing out on a chance to get to know her brother, his wife, and her nieces. I was certain there was a story there, but it hadn't been my place to ask.

All I could do was to make sure that everyone I loved knew how I felt, and that was a lesson I'd learned long ago. In the end, the love we shared was really all that we had, at least as far as I was concerned, and while I might never have a lot of money, there had never been a shortage of love in my life, and because of that, I considered myself the richest person I knew.

Chapter 7

"LET'S SEE. WHAT LOOKS good today?" Max, my ex-husband, asked me as he studied the display cases behind me.

"You know you're going to get two double-chocolate treats," I told him with a grin. "I thought your bride had you on a diet."

"It's not her, it's me. I've found that domestic bliss comes with an expanding waistline. Who knew Emily was such a great cook? She's feeding me as though I'm royalty."

"You don't deserve her. You know that, don't you?" I asked him, my smile broadening.

"Well, the truth of the matter is that I didn't deserve you either. Some guys are just born lucky, I guess."

"I'd say so," I said. "Say, did I see you talking to Nathan Billings last night? I didn't know you two knew each other."

"He tried out for a part in one of my plays, but he didn't get it," Max explained. He ran an amateur theater troupe in April Springs.

"Why not? Was he not good enough?" I asked as I filled Max's order without waiting for confirmation.

"No, he wasn't old enough," Max said with a grin. My ex's specialty was casting retirees in young roles, something that worked amazingly well. "He said that he was active in the theater group in Maple Hollow, but I told him that things ran a bit differently around here. I get it, though. Once you get a taste of being on stage, it's hard to let go of."

"I wouldn't know. Here are your donuts," I said as I handed him the bag.

He peeked inside. "Perfect." After he cinched the top of the bag, he said, "Do me a favor. If Emily asks you, I was never here."

"Max, we both know that I'm not about to lie to your wife for you. We've come a long way, but that's asking too much of me."

"Sorry," he said with that charming grin of his that I was now immune to forever.

"No apologies necessary," I said. After he paid, he took off, but not before stopping to salute me. Max hadn't been much of a husband, but he'd turned out to be a decent friend, which was more than I'd ever expected would happen when I'd caught him cheating on me.

Then again, that had been a very long time ago, and it didn't hurt that I for one was much happier with my life now than I'd ever been when I'd been married to Max. Sometimes things really did work out for the best.

There were only two customers in the donut shop at 10:45 when Jake came by. I hurried around the counter and hugged him fiercely. As I did, an older man named Kyle Wilkerson asked, "Where do we get in line for hugs? I never saw that on the menu."

Myrna Hollister, a contemporary of Kyle's, said, "Kyle, leave them be. Can't you see the woman is just glad to see her husband? You might know that if any woman had ever been fool enough to marry the likes of you."

Her words might have hurt a less confident man, but I knew from experience that the two of them lived to bicker with each other. It was almost a hobby for them.

"Myrna, you know I've never been one to settle down. Love them and leave them, I always say."

"Or just let them leave," she added.

"You know, your turn's about to come up again. What do you say? Want to have dinner with me again some night at the Boxcar Grill?"

Myrna blushed, which surprised me. Had the two of them actually gone out on a date at some point? She muttered, "In your dreams, Kyle Wilkerson."

As she hurried out, he said, "Or in yours. If that's the case, I'll see you tonight."

She faltered and then rushed out.

"That was just plain mean, even for you, Kyle," I said. "Are you about finished with that donut?"

"Just about," he said. "Sometimes Myrna forgets that we used to date in high school. I make it a point to remind her every now and then." Kyle ate the last of his donut, and then he patted Jake on the back on his way out.

"What do you make of that?" I asked.

"I didn't come by to waste my three spare minutes on Kyle and Myrna's ancient love life," Jake said. "I came to see my wife. Speaking of which, what was with that hug? I nearly lost my breath."

"Are you complaining, sir?" I asked him with a grin.

"Never. Just curious, that's all."

"All I can say is that I had a reminder this morning that life is short," I said by way of an explanation. I didn't want to get into what I'd heard about the Milner clan. I was sure I'd bring Jake up to speed about it later, but he was right. Now was our time.

"How goes the investigation?" I asked him after kissing him soundly.

Jake frowned for a moment before answering. "About that. The chief doesn't want us comparing notes."

"The two of you? That's not a very efficient use of police resources, is it?" I asked him.

"I'm talking about you and me, dear lady, as if you didn't know that already. I'm sorry, but he's worried that the state police are going to get involved, and he doesn't want to have to explain to them why a donut-maker is in the loop."

"Does that go both ways, or do you want to know what I've found out so far?" I asked him.

"As much as it pains me to say, you need to keep me in the dark, too," Jake answered. "If you want me to quit and come work with you, say the word, and it's done."

"I appreciate the gesture, but you're needed right where you are. I'll be okay. Phillip and I make a pretty good team, and we've got Momma as a resource, too. I'm sorry it's come to this."

"Me too, but it's his show, and I'm not about to try to tell him how to run it. Anyway, I just wanted to say hi and let you know where things stand. No hard feelings?"

I ignored his offered hand and kissed him soundly again. "Not between us."

"How about the chief?" Jake asked.

"He's a different story altogether," I replied. "Don't let it worry you. You and I are good, and that's really all that counts. Would you like a treat while you're here?"

"I'd better not. I'll be having lunch soon, and I don't want to spoil my appetite," he said as he walked over and grabbed the last apple fritter in the case.

"I understand. Would you like some coffee not to go with that, too?"

"No, I'm good. I've had so much this morning already that I'm getting the jitters. Sometimes I forget how much coffee it takes to run an investigation on the force," Jake said as he wolfed half the fritter down in short order.

"Well, don't stay too caffeinated," I told him. "Will I see you this afternoon?"

"I doubt it," Jake said, and then he finished the fritter and wiped his hands on a napkin. "Love you, Suzanne," he added as he walked to the door.

"Not half as much as I love you," I told him softly. I wasn't sure that he heard me, but he grinned and winked at me before he was gone.

At eleven on the nose, just as I was reaching to flip the OPEN sign to CLOSED, my partner in the investigation walked up.

"Am I early?" Phillip asked as I let him in before locking the door behind him.

"You're right on time for me to close the shop, but I still have work to do here before I'm ready to start digging into Lily's murder with you." He looked uncomfortable as I said the last bit. "Phillip Martin, what have you done?"

My stepfather looked at me and shook his head. "I swear it's your voice, but it's your mother's tone and cadence. Is it possible that scolding men is genetic in your family?"

"Highly likely when they deserve it, I believe. Don't try to change the subject. What have you been up to this morning? If we can't trust each other as partners, there's no use in us working together." I meant it, too. We were going to be putting our lives in each other's hands, and if I couldn't trust Phillip a thousand percent, it would be foolish, even reckless, to continue.

"Suzanne, I didn't go looking for information. Some just came my way by accident. I promise you that I'm telling the truth. I wouldn't do that to you."

He was clearly alarmed that I had been about to kick him off our team. Did digging into Lily's murder really mean that much to him? Maybe I'd overestimated just how much he missed his old job as our chief of police.

"Sorry. I might have overreacted. I meant what I said, though. I'm not ready to go."

"I can help you clean up," Phillip said by way of atonement.

"That's okay. You don't have to."

"Suzanne, like I told you last night, a broom fits my hand just as easily as it does yours. Tell me what to do, and I'll do it."

I could see that I wasn't going to win this argument, not that I really wanted to anyway. It didn't exactly get lonely working the shop by myself one day a week, but the cleanup always seemed to go faster when there were two of us. "Okay. Wipe the tables down with a damp rag, dry them with another, flip the stools over onto them, then sweep the floor out here."

"Wow, you didn't have any problem coming up with that list," he said with a grin, clearly happy that our little tiff was over.

"What can I say? It's a matter of ingrained muscle memory by now. In fact, I could make eighty percent of my donuts without my recipe book, but that doesn't mean that I'd ever want to lose it again." It had been stolen once upon a time and then burned in front of my cottage. Only Sharon, Emma's mother, had made a copy of it to study my recipes, so the work itself was saved, if not in its original form.

"I get that. Okay, you do your thing, and I'll do mine. By the way, where do you keep the clean rags?"

I got him set up, and then I started counting the money in the register as I ran the reports I needed. That could be a simple job or an arduous one, depending on how well I'd done during the course of the morning taking money and making change.

Thankfully, this time it balanced out to the penny. Once I had the deposit slip made out, I turned to find Phillip staring at me. "What's wrong? Do I have donuts in my hair or something?" As odd a thing as it was for me to ask, it had happened before.

"No. It's just that you're really good at this, aren't you?"

"It's not all that tough once you get the hang of it," I said.

"That describes every job that someone does well," my stepfather replied. "What else needs to be done?"

"I still have a pile of dishes in the kitchen that need to be washed, and I need to box up those donuts and clean the trays they are on, too."

"I can help with all of that," he volunteered. "Do you want to wash or dry?"

"I'll wash," I said. I wasn't about to turn him down. "Does Momma know that you can do dishes?" I asked him with a smile.

"She does," he admitted, "though evidently I'm not capable of putting dirty dishes in the dishwasher in the proper order and location."

"Don't worry about it. She doesn't like the way I do it either," I answered happily.

"Does Jake do it right?" he asked as we loaded the four dozen-odd donuts into boxes.

As I moved the trays into the kitchen, I said, "Jake and I have an agreement. He rinses them and puts them in the sink, and then I load them the way I like it to be done."

"Yeah, that's pretty much our system too," he answered.

As we started to wash and dry the pile of dishes, mugs, plates, pots, pans, and utensils, Phillip asked me, "I didn't want to say anything while you were working on your books, but can we talk now?"

"Absolutely. What did you find out this morning completely by accident?" Once he was finished updating me, I'd tell him about what Paige and Gabby had shared with me. It felt a bit like a double standard now that I thought about it. After all, *I* hadn't been looking for information either, but that hadn't kept me from taking advantage of the opportunities I'd had to uncover more about Lily Hamilton's murder while I'd been working at Donut Hearts.

"I was at the Boxcar, lingering over breakfast, when I overheard something that was interesting at another table. It seems that Nathan Billings isn't at all sure George can even be running the show now. At least that's what he told Travis Johnson. It sounded to me as though they were going to stage some kind of coup."

"Did you tell George?" I asked him.

"I tried calling him, but he didn't pick up."

"Don't worry about it. I've got his private number," I said as I dried off my hands and grabbed my cell phone.

The mayor picked up on the third ring.

"Suzanne, I don't want to hear any updates about Lily's murder investigation. I'm trying to stay out of it."

"That's not why I'm calling. You might not even care about the news I've got, but I'd never forgive myself if I didn't share it with you. You know what? Forget I even called. Have a nice day, *George*."

Phillip looked at me as though I'd lost my mind. "Suzanne, why didn't you tell him? Don't you think he deserves to at least hear what's going on?"

"You didn't hear his tone of voice, Phillip. If I had told him, he would have just ignored it."

"So we aren't even going to try?" My stepfather was clearly exasperated with me.

"If he doesn't call me back within thirty seconds, I'll eat every last one of those donuts we had left over today."

"That's not exactly a terrible punishment," Phillip said.

"Four dozen? Guess again."

I watched the clock, and when twenty-seven seconds passed without a phone call from the mayor, I began to regret my rash promise.

Fortunately, George didn't let me down.

"Okay, I'll bite. What is it?" he asked the second I said hello.

"Why, I'm just fine, thank you. How are you?"

"Peachy," the mayor said. "Talk."

"Phillip overheard Nathan Billings and Travis Johnson plotting an overthrow of your government at the Boxcar Grill this morning."

"You're kidding," George said. "Seriously? Do they think they can just waltz into my office and boot me out? What am I supposed to do, just stand there and watch?"

"I wasn't sure you wanted to even keep the job, given the circumstances," I told him.

"If I leave this office, it will be because of the voters, or because I decide to leave. *No one* is going to push me out. Do you hear me?"

His voice had gotten progressively louder as he'd spoken. "Hey, take it easy. I'm on your side, remember? Anyway, we thought you should know."

"Why didn't Phillip call me himself?" the mayor asked.

"He tried, but evidently you ignored his call," I said, giving him a little sass. After all, George and I could be salty with each other, especially when the moment called for it.

"Yeah, I did. Tell him I'm sorry," the mayor said.

"You can tell him yourself," I answered.

"I will, but I've got work to do right now. Thank him for me, would you? And thank you too, Suzanne. It's nice to know that you've still got my back."

"Always, Mr. Mayor," I said.

"Then it's not just George anymore?" he asked, referring to my earlier intentional use of his first name.

"When you act like a mayor, then that's what I call you," I said.

"You were right," Phillip said after I put my phone away. "Were you really going to eat all of those donuts?"

"Probably not, but I would have gone down swinging. It's a good thing, too. We can use them as bait to get our suspects to speak with us."

"Something tells me that you've done that before," Phillip said as he dove back into drying the dishes I'd washed so far.

"Are you kidding? It's like finding money on the ground," I told him. "So, while we're confessing things, I happened to overhear a few things myself this morning."

I waited for his rebuke, which honestly I richly deserved, but none came.

"What did you hear?"

"Aren't you going to say anything about me going rogue on you after I had a fit when I found out what you did?"

"I'd like to think that I'm too grown up to do that," he said, "but if it will make you feel better, shame on you," he added with a grin. "Now let's hear it."

I brought him up to speed on what I'd learned from Paige and Gabby, but I left out the news about the Milners. After all, we were looking into Lily Hamilton's murder, not gossiping about everything else going on in April Springs, at least not at the moment.

"Wow, I never would have imagined that Lily Hamilton would have such a diverse group of people who would want to see her dead."

"It's sobering at best, isn't it?" I asked him. "Who do you think the mysterious businessperson is with their own agenda? That's presuming that Gabby's right."

"I don't know, but I'm betting that Dot will have an inkling if anyone will," Phillip said.

When he made no move to call her, I asked him, "Would you like me to ask her?"

"No, but it can wait until we finish these dishes," Phillip said.

"Can it though?" I asked him.

"Fine, I'll call her right now," he said. He put the call on speaker so I could hear it as well. "Dot, I'm at the donut shop with Suzanne."

Before he could say more, she asked, "Why are you still there? She should have been closed ten minutes ago."

"I didn't know you kept up with my schedule," I said with a grin. "I'm just closing down for the day."

"What are you doing while she's working, Phillip?" Momma asked her husband.

"He started by wiping down the tables and then sweeping the floor in front. Now he's drying the dishes while I wash."

"Suzanne, your sense of humor eludes me most days," Momma said.

"It's true, though," Phillip said.

"Which part?"

"Every bit of it," my stepfather answered, clearly a touch put off by her unwillingness to believe that he'd pitch in.

Momma got it as well. "I apologize, and I applaud you for lending a hand. I assume this isn't a social call. What can I do for you both?"

"Momma, I heard that Lily was threatened by someone not long before she died, and it sounds as though it might be business related. Do you know any April Springs titans of industry who had a beef with our presumptive mayor-elect?"

"Not off the top of my head, but I can ask around," Momma said.

"Do it carefully, Dot," Phillip said. "We're dealing with a murderer here."

"I am not about to forget it," Momma said. "I hope the two of you are cognizant of that fact as well."

"Always," we said in unison.

"At least you both seem to be in sync. Carry on."

"We will," I said.

"Talk to you later, love," Phillip told his wife.

"I'm always here for you," she said. After their shared love was reaffirmed, Phillip put his phone away.

"Suzanne, did your mother seem surprised to you that I was helping out in the kitchen?" he asked me.

"I don't think it's going to rain today, but they're calling for it this weekend."

"Funny. I don't remember asking you for a weather report," Phillip said, "but I get it. You don't want to talk about it. After we finish up here, where should we go first?"

"I need to swing by the bank to make the deposit, but after that, I'm open to suggestions."

"Would it be too early to grab a bite to eat at the Boxcar first?" Phillip asked. "I know we don't have any suspects there, but I wouldn't mind grabbing something before we get started."

"That sounds good to me," I said. "Besides, you never know who might be there. Maybe we'll get lucky and someone on our list will be there too."

"And if they're not, we still get to eat early, so that's not exactly a tragedy, is it?"

"Not in my book," I said as I handed him the last plate. "Thanks for pitching in."

"Happy to do it," he said.

"Let me grab my deposit, and we can head over to the bank."

It wasn't to be though, at least not immediately.

As we were leaving Donut Hearts, one of our suspects was making their way toward us.

It appeared that lunch was going to have to wait after all.

Chapter 8

"ARE THOSE DONUTS SPOKEN for?" Jessie Carlton asked me as she hurried to us. "If not, I need to buy them from you."

"All of them?" I asked. "What's going on?"

"I'm having a memorial for Lily, and I need refreshments. Ever since Patty Cakes closed, the only other choice around here is the grocery store, and Lily *hated* their bakery. Your donuts aren't ideal, but they're the best I can do on such short notice."

"There's a decent bakery in Union Square," I said. "I'm sure they would be happy to take care of you. You should try them." I didn't really have any plans for my day's surplus other than using them as bribes for our suspects, but I didn't like Jessie's attitude. After all, I had a sign up in my shop that said I could refuse service to anyone I pleased, and besides, we weren't even in the shop at that point.

"I'm sure Suzanne would love to help you," Phillip said appeasingly. "Wouldn't you?" he asked me as he turned to face me and gave me a stern look.

He was right. I couldn't afford to let a little perceived slight stop me from doing the right thing. After all, Lily had been a resident of April Springs, and she deserved the best at her memorial. That meant, at least as far as I was concerned, treats from Donut Hearts. "Of course. I would be happy to let you have them," I said.

"Thank you," Jessie said, the relief clear in her voice. "I'm sorry if I was a bit snippy earlier. Your donuts really are delicious."

"I like to think so, but I'm glad that you agree," I said.

"How much do I owe you? I'll take them all."

"Tell you what. I'll donate them to the cause if Phillip and I can come and pay our respects, too. How does that sound?"

My stepfather looked at me oddly for a second, but then he caught on quickly enough. We might have to delay our lunch plans indefinitely, but this was too good an opportunity to pass up. With any luck, at least some of our suspects would be on hand at the wake, including Jessie herself.

"I'm afraid that's not possible," she said, much to my surprise. "It's nothing personal, but this will just be folks who worked on Lily's mayoral campaign. Given that you two were George Morris's biggest advocates, it wouldn't be right."

She had a point, given the circumstances. I couldn't deny it: I had been George's biggest supporter, and Phillip and Momma hadn't been far behind.

"I hope you understand," she said.

"We do," I answered. "How are you coping with the loss of your friend? You must be devastated."

"I'm keeping myself busy," she said. "Honestly, it hasn't sunk in yet. There's so much to do now that Lily is gone. I've been asked to fill in for her in several of our groups. I feel as though I don't really have any choice. Lily would have wanted it that way."

"I believe if Lily had her druthers, she'd still be with us," I said. I shouldn't have been so insensitive, but I couldn't stand the way Jessie was clearly reveling in her new role, or roles, as the case might be.

"Of course," she said dismissively. "Now, about those donuts."

"They're yours," I said, feeling bad that I'd just taken a shot at her without much provocation.

"Excellent. Will fifty dollars cover the bill?"

"No," I said.

"What?" Phillip and Jessie said simultaneously.

"How much do you want, Suzanne? You've obviously got me right where you want me. I should warn you, though..."

"Don't finish that thought, or I might change my mind," I said. "What I meant to say was that they are on the house. I might not have been on Lily's team in the mayoral election, but she was one of us. Please accept these as a goodwill gesture."

Jessie looked pleased, and so did Phillip. Did they both really think that I was going to gouge the woman for a *memorial* service? I felt bad as it was. The donuts had been sitting in my display case all day, unclaimed and unwanted. Sure, they would be fresh enough for just about everyone else in the world, and no one would know they weren't just recently made but me, but still, I felt a little bad about it.

"Thank you," Jessie said. "It's most kind of you. If there's anything I can do in return, just name it, Suzanne."

"Where were you just before they found Lily?" Phillip asked her.

She looked shocked by the question, and a bit flustered. "I'm sure that I was with our group of supporters planning the new mayor's inauguration in the basement."

"I didn't see you there," Phillip said.

"Funny, but I didn't either," I added.

She looked positively trapped. "I may have stepped away for a few minutes to get a breath of fresh air, but I can assure you, it wasn't more than that."

"Of course, Lily was found pretty close to City Hall," I said. If Jessie was gone even five minutes, it would still have given her time to confront Lily, clobber her with the ballot box, and still make it back before anyone else was any the wiser.

"She was," Jessie said. "I can take those from you, if you'd like."

She tried to get the boxes out of my hands, but I held on tightly. "That's okay. We're happy to walk you to your car."

Jessie gave up, since the only way to wrestle them from me would be a full frontal attack.

"When was the last time you saw her alive?" Phillip asked her. There was more of the old cop in his voice than the current civilian, though he hadn't been on the force for some time.

"It must have been at least an hour before the winner was due to be announced," Lily said.

"Wow, that's kind of unusual," I said. We were nearing her Subaru, and she hit the hatchback release before we got there, no doubt hoping to get my donuts and be on her way without us getting in any more questions. That wasn't going to happen if I could help it.

"What's so unusual about it?" she asked me.

"Everyone in town knows that you were by Lily's side during the entire campaign," I said. "Doesn't it seem strange that you wouldn't be with her for the entire hour before the election results were about to be announced?"

"The work was finished. Win or lose, I'd done my part," she said. "Besides, Lily told me that she had two meetings before the results were announced. I offered to go with her, but she was adamant about doing it alone."

"Who were the meetings with?" Phillip asked her.

"One was with Ally Tucker, but she wouldn't tell me who the other one was with." After a few moments of hesitation, she added, "I think it was a man."

"Why would she need to meet with Ally?" I asked her. Ally Tucker was a local realtor and amateur actress, a small woman barely five feet tall, and if she weighed a hundred pounds, it would have to be soaking wet. Was it even possible for a woman of her size to hit Lily over the head, let alone lift the ballot box in the first place? I doubted it, but we'd still need to follow up and speak with her. Then again, Ally was known for cutting corners and playing on the wrong side of the street whenever it suited her, so there might just be something there after all.

"I have no idea," Jessie said as we got to her car. I'd been dragging my feet getting there, but short of walking backward, it had been inevitable.

"Lily might not have said the man's name she was meeting, but you were one of her best friends," I said, laying it on thick. "Surely you suspect someone."

"I wasn't *one* of her best friends. I was her *only* best friend," Jessie said adamantly.

That was what Gabby had told me, too. "Then you should know who she was seeing in secret, shouldn't you?"

"It wasn't anything like that," Jessie said. "After Lily's unfortunate period dating George Morris, she'd sworn off men for good, at least romantically."

"So you believe," I said.

"So I know, Suzanne!"

Wow, she really took that personally. Was it because she'd been excluded by Lily, or could it be that she was telling us the truth, at least as much of it as she knew?

"I'm sorry. I didn't mean to doubt your word," I apologized almost automatically. "I know you two were close."

"We were like sisters," she said, accepting my apology with alacrity. "Thank you again for the donuts, but I'm sure you understand why I can't invite you both."

"We get it," Phillip said. "Who all is going to be there, anyway?"

"Just her supporters, and maybe a few other folks as well," Jessie hedged as she shut the hatchback and got into her car.

As she drove away, Phillip said, "That woman is lying about something."

"I got the same feeling too, but which part? Did she really see Lily closer to the time when she was murdered than she admitted to us? Did she know who the mystery man was that Lily was supposedly meeting? Or was it something as simple as just wanting to exclude us from the memorial service by lying about who would really be there?"

"That was a class move donating your donuts, by the way," Phillip said.

"Hey, I've got a big heart," I said. "It's even in my name."

He smiled softly. "No matter the reason, we're not finished with Jessie Carlton."

"No, clearly we're not," I said as I headed back to my Jeep, which was still parked in front of Donut Hearts. "As an added bonus, we can add Ally Tucker to our list as well."

"And let's not forget the mystery man Lily was meeting right before the announcement," Phillip said. "Do you think that it was just business, or was there something more personal about it, despite what Jessie just told us?"

"I don't know, but let's hope we figure it out sooner rather than later. I hate this cloud hanging over George's head."

"We're doing everything we can," Phillip said. "In the meantime, let's go get that lunch."

"First the bank, and then the Boxcar," I reminded him. "Business before pleasure."

"You've got a one-track mind, young lady," Phillip said as he got into the passenger side of the Jeep.

"It's my business," I said as I got in and started it. "I have to be that way."

"Like mother, like daughter," he said.

"You do realize that's the best compliment you could pay me," I said with a smile as I drove us to the bank.

"I know. That's why I said it," he answered with a grin of his own.

"Can't we drop this off in the night deposit and be on our way?" Phillip asked me as I parked my Jeep in front of the bank.

"No, I need a receipt for the deposit right away. It's a quirk I have, and before you ask, I can't use the drive-up window, either. They don't take coins, and you'd be amazed by how many people use their spare change to buy donuts."

"I wouldn't be amazed at all," Phillip said. "Why don't you go on in, and I'll wait out here for you. How does that sound?"

"It sounds as though you're going to do some investigating without me," I said as I made no move to get out of my vehicle.

"I'm just going to make a few phone calls, Suzanne. I'll tell you anything I find out, if there's anything *to* find out, as soon as you're back."

"You'd better," I said with a smile.

"Do I look crazy enough to lie to *any* of the Hart women?" he asked me earnestly.

"No, now that you mention it, you don't. I shouldn't be long."

"Look at the parking lot. I've got a feeling this isn't going to be as fast as you think it is."

I looked around and saw that he was right. Normally I had the bank mostly to myself when I dropped off my deposit, but then again, I usually made it there before the folks with regular jobs got off on their lunch hours. Having Phillip "help" me had set me back a bit. Oh well. It wasn't as though I was some kind of pretty princess. I could stand in line with the best of them.

There were only two tellers working, despite seven people wanting to do their banking ahead of me. I was heading for the shortest line when I happened to notice Ally Tucker standing in the longer of the two lines. She was tapping her right foot impatiently as she watched the line move not at all. I for one was happy with the lack of progress. It would give me the perfect opportunity to grill her about Lily Hamilton's murder. I felt a bit of a twinge excluding Phillip, but he'd chosen to stay in the Jeep. I hadn't forced him. Besides, I'd share with him as soon as I was finished.

If we got lucky, maybe he'd have something new to share, too.

"It looks as though everyone decided to come to the bank at the same time," I said to Ally as I leaned forward. She really was a little bit of a woman, but I knew from experience with demure women never to underestimate them. After all, though Momma looked positively towering compared to Ally, to most folks, she was tiny herself. Ally's hair caught my attention. Had she dyed it auburn? I'd always thought of it as a bit of a brassy brown, but there were definitely hues in her new coif that weren't found in nature.

"I've got to drop off a due-diligence check and meet my buyers in twenty minutes," she said impatiently.

"This shouldn't take more than five or ten of those," I said.

"The meeting is in Union Square," she said.

"Then you're not going to make it," I said. She couldn't have gotten there with a jet pack or a rocket car. Where were those things, anyway? When I'd been a kid, they'd promised us all kinds of cool things the future would hold, but I was still waiting.

"Obviously," she said with a snap in her voice.

"Sorry," I said. "I didn't mean to butt in." Ha. That was exactly what I'd meant to do, but it wouldn't hurt putting her on the defensive.

I was about to say something about Lily when Ally interrupted me. "No, I'm the one who needs to apologize. Sometimes I let my impatience get the better of me. Sorry about that."

"Of course," I said. What was up with Ally Tucker? I'd never known her to apologize in her life. She pulled out her phone and bumped her appointment half an hour as we stood there in line.

"Great. They're getting cold feet," she said as she ended her call and put her phone away. "And why shouldn't they? They're buying a house they can't afford to impress people who don't even like them. I tried to tell them they were going to be house poor, but they wouldn't listen." She paused and then grinned at me. "Okay, full disclosure, I didn't try all that hard. I'm going to take a trip with the commission I get on this sale."

"Are you really going to leave town?" I asked her. "What about Lily Hamilton's murder? Don't you want to stick around and find out who did it?" *Smooth, Suzanne*, I said to myself. There was nothing like being subtle. Then again, there wasn't much subtle about the woman I was speaking with. Maybe she was already rubbing off on me.

"That's one of the main reasons I'm going," she said softly. "Lily's death has made me realize how short life is."

I couldn't disagree with the sentiment, but I was still surprised to hear her professing it, especially given what I'd heard about their relationship. "It must have especially shaken you," I told her as the line moved up one person.

"Why do you say that?" Ally asked me as she pivoted around and stared at me.

"I heard you were one of the last people to see her alive," I said. "You two had a meeting outside of City Hall not long before her body was found."

"What are you implying?" Ally asked me curtly.

"Nothing," I said. "What was so important that you had to meet with her minutes before the election results were due to be announced?"

"We were working on something together," she said. Ally was being vague, clearly hoping that I'd drop it.

Did the woman not know me at all?

"Really? What were you working on?"

"Business," Ally told me, and then in a louder voice, she asked, "Could you get someone else to help us, too?"

"Sorry. Everyone else is at lunch," the man behind the teller's window told her. I didn't think he was sorry at all. In fact, it appeared to me that it was taking every ounce of self-discipline he had not to laugh out loud.

"Fine," she said.

Ally tried to ignore me, but I wasn't about to let that happen. When she didn't turn back around despite me clearing my throat three times, I tapped her on the shoulder. "You know, I've had an excellent year. Maybe I could invest it, if you're looking for new money."

I couldn't have afforded to invest in a meal out given my receivables as of late, but she didn't have to know that.

Ally shook her head. "Sorry, but the deal died with her. It was a stab in the dark anyway."

"Still, you must be crushed," I said. "Seeing how you two were so close." The last bit was a dig, and she knew it.

"I'm not saying that we were BFFs or anything close to that, but Lily and I understood each other. We were equals. Honestly, I'm better off now that the deal is gone. It frees up my capital for some other investment ventures I've been considering that are going to be much more lucrative. I just hate that it happened that way. As to being the last person to see her alive, she was meeting a man right after we got together. He's the one they should be looking for." I wasn't sure who she was trying to convince, herself or me, but I didn't have time to push her any harder.

"Do you have any idea who it might have been?" I asked her.

"It could have been anybody. She didn't tell me, and I didn't ask. I left her waiting for him, and the next thing I heard was that she was dead. It's all very tragic." She sounded sincere enough, but then again, she'd sounded the same way when she'd just talked with her clients. Who knew what she was really like down deep inside?

Ally finally reached the teller window.

I tried to listen in, or even get a glimpse of the check to see if she'd been telling the truth, but she was too cagy for me. She did her banking—depositing the check and withdrawing some money as well—and then she pulled out her phone and pretended to talk to someone as she walked past me.

I had a new question for Momma. What was this mysterious business deal Ally had with Lily Hamilton? Did it hinge on her becoming mayor, or was it related to something else? I'd have to ask Momma to do a little more digging for us. If something was in the air, she'd have a whiff of it soon enough.

"Did you happen to see who was in there with you?" Phillip asked as I walked out of the bank. He'd left the passenger seat of my Jeep and was leaning against the front bumper.

"I saw, we spoke. More to follow," I said as I gestured for him to get back in my vehicle. Once we were both in our seats, I brought him up to date. After I had, I asked him, "Did she tell *you* anything?"

"What makes you think I spoke with her?" Phillip asked cagily.

"Come on, you weren't outside enjoying the fresh air. Spill, Chief."

I rarely called him Chief anymore, and it caught him a bit off guard. "I tried," he admitted sheepishly, "but she blew me off."

"Don't beat yourself up about it," I said, doing my best to console him. "By the time you got to her, I had her pretty steamed. What do you think she was really meeting with Lily about?"

"I don't know. Let's call your mother and see if she has any idea."

"Fine. You call while I drive. I'm starving."

"Great minds think alike," he said with a grin.

Momma didn't have any idea about Lily and Ally either, but she'd dig into it. In the meantime, she was still trying to fill our first request, and as they were speaking, I could hear her say, "I've got another call I have to take. Bye."

He barely got out a farewell of his own before the call ended.

"She's going to look into it," Phillip said.

"Excellent. Did you have any luck while I was multitasking in the bank?"

"I left a few messages, but no, my calls were all a bust." It clearly hurt him to admit it.

"Well, at least we finally get to eat now," I said.

If only that had turned out to be true.

Chapter 9

"SUZANNE, I NEED TO speak with you. It's urgent."

"Ray, I can't imagine us sharing the same definition of that word. What's urgent to you isn't necessarily urgent to me." The newspaperman had a habit of turning up at the worst possible time, but I still had to be polite to him, within reason. After all, I needed to be nice to the man for Emma and Sharon's sake.

"Trust me. You're going to want to hear this," he said.

I kept walking.

Phillip didn't, though.

"Come on. I'm hungry," I told my stepfather.

"Let's at least hear what the man has to say," Phillip said.

"Did you feel that way when you were the chief of police?" I asked him.

"No, but I never claimed to be perfect, then or now. Come on. What could it hurt?"

I could see that arguing with my stepfather wasn't going to do me any good, so I turned back to Ray Blake. "You have one minute to intrigue me."

"You know what? Forget it. I don't appreciate your tone, Suzanne."

"Believe me, I've heard that before," I said. He was right, though. If we were going to stop and talk to him, the least I could do was be nicer than I was being. I blamed it on hunger, that and a history of bad experiences with the man, but that was still no excuse. "Ray, I'm sorry I was so snippy. I haven't eaten in ages, and I tend to get a bit salty when I'm starving. What's up?"

It took him eight seconds to decide to accept my apology, which was a good thing, since I was only going to allow him ten. "I have two leads for you about Lily Hamilton's murder."

Ray was famous for his conspiracy theories and outlandish notions. I had been right. This was all one colossal waste of time.

I was about to tell him just that when Phillip spoke up. "Come on then, Ray. Don't make us drag it out of you. What are you talking about?"

"These aren't just wild speculations," he protested. "I have reasons to believe that either hypothesis might be true."

"Why come to us then, Ray? Why not publish what you know?"

"I have my reasons," the newspaperman said furtively.

"Did you tell Chief Grant?" the former police chief asked.

"I tried, but he wouldn't listen to me, and neither would Jake," he said, looking hard at me for the last bit.

"What did you try to tell them?" I asked, refusing to rise to the bait. My husband was a grown man. If Ray felt as though he needed an apology from him, he'd have to ask for it himself, not that I believed for one second that he'd get one.

"Did you know that Lily Hamilton was having problems with the Mob?" he asked us softly as he looked all around us.

"Seriously? Like from *The Godfather*?" I asked him. "Lily?"

"I discovered that in exchange for her election, she promised some rather shady characters from Charlotte that certain things would be overlooked when it came to a certain development deal on the outskirts of town. Do you follow me?"

"I don't," I said bluntly. "Can't you be a little more specific than that?"

"I can, but I've grown partial to my legs, and I don't want them broken," he said.

"But you're not afraid to jeopardize ours," I said.

"Hey, I just thought you might like some help. I know that you two are digging into what happened to our brand-spanking-new mayor, so don't bother denying it."

I looked at him and grinned for a moment before I spoke. "No comment."

"Why am I not surprised? Anyway, do you want to hear my second theory or not?"

"Sure, why not?" I asked.

"Lily's love life had gotten rather messy of late. Evidently she took George Morris's rejection to heart, and in a weak moment, she reached out to a former beau who is a genuinely bad guy. She broke it off with him, but he wouldn't accept the rejection. I know for a fact that he was in town last night. I saw him with my own eyes."

"What's his name?" Phillip asked him.

"You can have it, in exchange for a promise," Ray said smugly.

"You're not getting my firstborn, and I'm not even pregnant," I said. "Come on, Phillip. Let's eat before all of the day's specials are gone. I don't even care what Trish is serving. I'm hungry enough to eat two of them all by myself."

"All I want is an exclusive after you find the killer," Ray said.

"We can't promise that even if we manage to discover who murdered Lily. Ray, we can't make the killer sit down and talk to you."

"I'm not talking about them," Ray explained. "I want your story, Suzanne."

"My story? You're kidding. I don't have a story."

"Who exactly are you trying to kid now? You've done this enough to get attention outside of April Springs, and I know with the right slant, I can make your story nationwide. You'll be famous. Isn't that exciting?"

"I'd rather have a root canal while someone's hitting me in the stomach with a wet fish," I said. "No deal, Ray."

"Fine, but you'll never find this guy without me. I'm willing to bet that not even Gabby Williams knows about the affair. Lily was so circumspect about dating this guy that *no one* is going to know his name."

"I'll take that bet," I said. "Thanks for the information," I added. Ray looked so upset that I decided to throw him a bone. "If everything works out, and I mean everything, I might give you something, on one condition."

"No one gets story approval of my newspaper," he said defiantly. "No one."

"I don't care what you write, but if there's even the slightest whiff of my name attached to it, what I do for a living, where I live, or what I'm about to eat for lunch, I'm coming after you, Ray."

"You can't threaten the free press, Suzanne."

"I'm not. I'm just going to have a chat with your wife and your daughter, and I have a hunch that they'll see my side of it. Do you really want to risk alienating the two most important women in your life over a *story*?"

The man turned absolutely pale at the mention of my threat. "Understood. His name is Franklin Kinder. He lives in Union Square. He's an attorney with a mean streak, so be careful, you two."

"Thanks, Ray. As always, it was a pleasure."

As we walked up the steps to the Boxcar Grill, Phillip said, "That man was absolutely terrified, wasn't he?"

"And not of the Mob," I said. "Think about it. I know how brave you are, but how would you like both Momma *and* me angry with you at the same time?"

He shivered at the very thought of it. "No, thank you."

I surprised my stepfather by reaching out and squeezing his shoulder, the closest I could get to hugging him, as we reached the door. "Don't worry. You'd have to do something monumentally stupid for that to ever happen, and you're not reckless by any means."

"I appreciate that," Phillip said as he held the door open for me.

I was glad that I hadn't laughed at his reaction.

After all, the threat was real enough, and I had a hunch that I'd *never* have to follow through, with either Phillip or Ray.

"What's going on?" I asked Trish as I looked around the Boxcar. Not only was every table taken, but nearly every seat was as well.

"What can I say? It helps to run the only real restaurant in town that serves lunch."

"I know that," I said, "but I've *never* seen it this crowded."

"It happens sometimes. It's as though everyone decides to eat lunch at the same time. I'm not complaining. It's doing wonders for my bottom line."

I looked around and saw Millie Florian sitting with Bee Westmore. "*Bee and Millie* are sharing a table? You're kidding me. Peter's ears must be on fire, wherever he is." Peter had been married to Millie when he'd met Bee, and he'd dumped his wife for his new girlfriend. Then, not four years later, he had jettisoned her, too, this time in favor of a much younger version of the other women. "How are they getting along?"

"Since Peter got rid of Bee too, there's been a great deal less animosity between the two women," Trish said. "It doesn't surprise me. After all, they have a great deal in common."

"That's true, much more than the fact that they were both once with Peter," I said. Phillip was taking it all in, not adding to the conversation, but in his defense, I had a feeling he was still thinking about my comments earlier. I'd have to go out of my way to show how much I cared for him. After all, if he was going to be my investigation partner, it wouldn't do to have him tiptoeing around me.

I was about to say something when I saw the door open behind me, and in one of those moments of pure karma that life sometimes gives you, the man in question himself walked in, with his younger paramour on his arm no less.

"This ought to be good," Trish said with a smile as she looked on. "I just wish we had some popcorn."

Peter took a few steps in, and while his younger girlfriend was studying the room, looking for a table, he saw his exes sitting together. "Come on, Viv. We're going to eat someplace else."

"But you promised me the Boxcar," she said with a whiny pout that would have driven me up the wall in no time. Then again, I wasn't vulnerable to that figure of hers, so maybe he had his reasons.

"I can do better than that, baby," he said as he turned back toward the door in order to make his escape.

Phillip must have seen him leaving, because he chose that moment to stumble against the door, effectively blocking his way as Millie and Bee got up together and headed toward us.

"Get out of my way, fool! I need to leave," he told Phillip forcefully.

"Sorry. I lost my balance for a second. I just need a minute to catch my breath," he said, pretending to be an old man in less than peak physical condition. I knew for a fact that there was nothing wrong with Phillip's balance or his breath, and I grinned at him, but only after making sure that Peter couldn't see it.

"Peter, we'd like a word with you," Millie said as they approached.

"More than just one," Bee told him.

Phillip softened then and moved away from the door. Peter didn't waste any time exiting, leaving Viv behind as collateral damage.

"Hey, I know you. You were Peter's wife," Viv said, and then she glanced over at Bee. "And you were his girlfriend."

"Viv, why don't you pull up a seat to our table? One's just opening up, and there's a lot we have to talk about."

"I don't know if that's such a good idea. I'm supposed to be having lunch with Peter," she said, looking confused by the aggressive friendliness of the two older women.

"It appears that he's already left you," Bee said. "Seriously, we won't bite. Come on. It will be fun."

I wasn't sure about that, but another table opened up, and I started to guide Phillip toward it after we ordered two specials from Trish. Our table happened to have four chairs, and Bee grabbed one of ours and added it to their small table.

"You were out of breath *and* lost your balance at the same time?" I asked Phillip after Trish had cleared the table and took our orders.

"Hey, it happens to the best of us," he replied with a broad smile.

"I applaud the sentiment, but why did you go easy on him and let him leave?" I asked.

"I didn't want the bloodshed to ruin everyone's lunch," he replied.

"What do you think is going on over there?"

"From the way Viv's face is going paler and paler, I've got a hunch she's getting an education about her current beau," I said.

"Speaking of beaus, what do you think of Ray's scenarios? The Mob? Seriously? And what about this Franklin Kinder? I've never heard of him."

"Neither have I, but that doesn't mean that there's nothing there. In my experience, some of the things Ray Blake believes have kernels of truth at their hearts. While the Mob might not be after control of April Springs, there could be a bad guy trying to circumvent the rules by putting pressure on the mayor. As to Kinder, I'd like to check him out and see what he has to say for himself."

"We can put him on our list," Phillip said.

"But he's not our first priority."

"Who is?" Phillip asked.

I was saved from answering by Trish showing up with two plates heaped with meat loaf, mashed potatoes and gravy, and green beans. There were two biscuits on a separate plate, and after she'd put the food down, she grabbed a pitcher of sweet tea and refilled our glasses, which we'd gotten before we sat down. As she did, she bent forward and asked softly, "Did you two just see that?"

"See what?" I asked as I looked around the room. The only really odd thing was the triumvirate of Peter's conquests, and nothing had really changed there.

"Good old Sneaky Pete just grabbed a look inside. You should have seen his face when he realized that his precious little Viv was having lunch with Millie and Bee."

"Trish, have I ever told you that you've got a wicked streak a mile wide?" I asked her with a grin. "Maybe that's why we've always been such good friends."

"We're kindred spirits," Trish agreed.

After she was gone, I took a taste of the meat loaf. It was amazing, maybe even better than Momma's, which was saying something indeed. I'd never tell her that, though. There were some secrets that were worth protecting, no matter what.

"I'm still waiting for an answer," Phillip said after taking a bite of his own food. "Who's number one, Suzanne?"

"I was thinking we could start with Mercy Host and find out what she was looking for so frantically near the crime scene," I admitted. "It's driving me crazy."

"Do you think she'll really tell us?" he asked after stabbing a few green beans and eating them. Back in the kitchen, Hilda added something to them that I'd never been able to place, and they were absolutely amazing. I'd asked her more than once, but all she'd do was smile. I couldn't blame her. There were some special donut flavorings I used that not even Emma and Sharon knew about. After all, I was entitled to a couple of gems all to myself.

"Probably not, but I'm curious to see how she reacts when she finds out that her little search wasn't all that surreptitious."

"That's fair," he said and then took another bite of biscuit. "And then?"

"Some of that depends on what we learn from Mercy," I said, wiping up a bit of gravy with a biscuit bite. Momma would probably have been appalled by my lack of manners and couth, but if Phillip minded, he didn't say anything. Besides, there wasn't much better than gravy and biscuits as far as combinations went, at least in the savory end of the spectrum.

"If that's a dead end, though?" he persisted.

"Then we head to Union Square and see if we can get Mr. Kinder to spend a little time with us," I said. "Don't ask me what comes after that. I'm making this up as I go along. You knew that about me, right?"

He laughed. "What, do you mean that there isn't some detailed and intricate plan you've got for us to find the killer?"

I didn't even smile. "What can I say? I like to see where the leads I uncover take me."

His laughter died in his throat. "That's the best way to investigate. I was just giddy on gravy and sweet tea. I didn't mean anything by it, Suzanne."

Great. I'd been planning to try to make him feel more at ease with me, and instead, I'd just made him a bit leerier than he'd been before. Reaching across the table, I touched his hand lightly. "We're a good team, Phillip. You remind me of Jake with the methodical way you attack a problem. I like to think I offer a nice counterbalance with my intuitive streaks."

I knew that comparing him in any way to my husband would make him feel good. He respected Jake not only as a man but as a police officer too. "Good enough," he said as we finished up.

I reached for the check Trish had dropped off, but he beat me to it. "This one's on me."

"You don't have to pay for my food every time we eat out somewhere," I said.

"You're not going to rob me of the pleasure of telling your mother that I took her favorite daughter out to lunch, are you?" he asked.

"Well, as far as that goes, we both know that I'm her *only* daughter—her only child for that matter—but that's beside the point."

He just kept looking at me with that expression of silent request, and I had no choice but to fold. "What I meant to say was thank you for the meal."

"You are most welcome," he said with a smile as he left Trish a much-too-generous tip.

Just as a change of pace, I decided to keep my mouth shut and not comment on it.

After all, we were just getting back on good footing, and I didn't want to do anything to jeopardize it.

It was time to track down Mercy and see what she had to say for herself.

As we walked out, I turned to see that Millie, Bee, and Viv were deep in conversation, and it didn't take a genius to know what, or more pointedly, who the topic of conversation was.

If I were Peter, I'd get in my car and keep driving until I hit water, on one coast or the other.

Chapter 10

"HI, MERCY," I SAID as she answered the door of her house. It was a true brick McMansion, with stately columns, large expansive windows bracketed by white shutters, and a well-manicured lawn. Mercy had married well—and divorced even better, as I'd heard her boast before. She was an attractive woman, her striking good looks just starting to fade. It was clear that she had counted on riding her appearance instead of her personality, and she was starting to come up short.

"Hello, Donut Lady," she said drolly, and then she spotted Phillip and smiled instantly. "Why, if it isn't the chief of police. How are you, Chief Martin?"

"I've been retired for quite a while now," he said, obviously flustered by Mercy's elevated attention. I'd known women like her all my life, cool to other females but not to the men they met. Why would *anyone* want to alienate half the world's population? I myself tried my best to get along with men and women both, and in my opinion, anyone worth their salt felt the same way.

"That's hard to imagine. You just keep getting more handsome with every year," she said, slathering it on a little too thick, at least in my opinion.

"My mother, his wife, thinks so, too," I interjected before things got even more awkward. "Mercy, we'd like to talk to you about Lily Hamilton."

"Tragic, wasn't it? Cut down so young in life."

Lily hadn't exactly been a schoolgirl, but I could see Mercy's point. The older I got, the more I felt as though anyone who died before their hundredth birthday felt like they were taken before their time, as ridiculous as that sounded. "It was. You two were at odds quite a bit, weren't you?"

Mercy still hadn't invited us in, which was a bit of a slight, given her Southern upbringing. Then again, Phillip and I weren't exactly social climbers, so maybe she felt justified treating us like commoners.

"We had a friendly rivalry. It was all quite innocent," she said. From what I'd heard about their relationship, I couldn't believe she could even keep a straight face saying it.

"Really? That's not what I hear," I said.

"Suzanne, you honestly should know better than to believe everything you hear through the gossip channels of April Springs. I thought your mother raised you better than that."

Wow, I must have struck a nerve. The way I knew that was that she'd brought up my mother to slam me, but I decided to let it go. "Mercy, what were you looking for in the tall grass after Lily was murdered?" I asked her.

She looked startled by the question, and before she could compose herself, Phillip added, "It was just after the police released the crime scene, so it must have been important. What exactly did you lose, Mercy?"

"I'm sure I don't know what you're talking about," she said huffily.

"Really? You're going to try to play it that way? That's odd, because we have an eyewitness who is willing to swear to it in court under oath." I hadn't cleared that with Paige, but I knew she wouldn't let me down. If it came down to it, she was in my corner, and I was in hers.

"What concern is it of yours, anyway?" Mercy asked, ducking our statement. "Chief, as you pointed out, you are no longer serving as our police chief, and Suzanne, as far as I know, you've *never* been in law enforcement at all."

"I might be retired, but I still volunteer my services to the department on occasion," Phillip said.

"And you?" she asked as she turned to me.

"I'm looking out for my friend, the mayor."

Mercy gave me a sidelong look. "Odd, but I was under the impression that he lost the race."

"That was just a preliminary count. There's no doubt in my mind that when the rest of the ballots are counted, he'll win his old job back easily," I said. Whether it was true or not, I was mainly just trying to get a reaction from Mercy.

Boy, did I ever get one.

The look on her face was shock, plain and simple. "I'm so sorry, but I'm late for an appointment. I really must be going," she said hurriedly, and then she stepped back into her house and did everything but slam the door in our faces.

"We struck a nerve there, didn't we?" I asked Phillip as we walked back to my Jeep. "She didn't answer a single question we asked her, at least not truthfully, did she?"

"She's clearly upset about something. I'm just not sure it was about Lily's murder," Phillip agreed. "What a bunch of hooey she was spouting. Mercy always was one to lay it on too thick."

"You seemed a bit flustered," I told him as I started the vehicle.

"I never know how to handle it when people talk that way," the former chief said. "It's embarrassing."

I decided to let that one ride. After all, I was still struggling to get back on good terms with my stepfather, so I didn't want to rock the boat any more than I had to. "Did you see her face when I said that George won the election after all?"

"We caught her totally off guard," Phillip said. "If she hated Lily so much, why would she even care if she were elected or not? It doesn't matter now anyway, but even if it did, it just doesn't make sense. I wish I could haul her into the station and get some straight answers out of her."

"Remember, all we have at our disposal are charm and guile," I reminded him. "That makes it a bit harder."

"I know. The problem is that I'm not so sure either one of us is overloaded in the charm department."

I grinned at him. "Maybe not, but we both have more than our share of guile."

He smiled back. "I won't disagree with that. What do we do about Mercy? I have a feeling that what she was searching for is going to be crucial in finding the killer."

"Does that mean that you think that she did it?" I asked him as I headed toward Union Square to see the attorney recently added to our list.

"Not necessarily, but it must be connected somehow. Why else would Mercy risk being seen doing something so suspicious at the scene of a murder?"

"I don't know, but we'll find out."

"Just not anytime soon," Phillip said gruffly.

"Don't forget, we're just getting started. I have faith in us. Let's let her simmer a bit, and then we'll speak with her again later," I said. "For now, we need to speak with Franklin Kinder. After that, if we still have time, I'd like to have another run at Nathan Billings and Travis Johnson."

"That's a lot on our plates," Phillip said.

"Then we'd better be quick about it," I replied.

"Mr. Kinder, we appreciate you seeing us on such short notice," I said as we walked into the lawyer's office in Union Square. Not only had there not been any clients present, but there was no staff either. I wasn't at all certain how successful an attorney he was, but maybe he didn't generally deal with walk-in clients.

"Of course. I have a few minutes before I have to be in court," he said officiously. "What is this in regard to?"

"Your relationship with Lily Hamilton," Phillip said rather abruptly. I'd been about to lead into it gently before I started asking tough questions, but evidently my stepfather had taken the man at his word. He wanted this to be brief, so that was exactly what he was going to get.

"I'm sorry?" he asked.

"We are, too. It's a shame about what happened to Lily, especially after she just dumped you again," I said. It felt good being so bold. Maybe there was something to be said for the direct approach after all.

"I'm not sure what you *think* you know, but I can assure you that our parting was mutual. She called me out of the blue recently, and after a long conversation about the problems we'd had in the past, we *both* decided that we'd be better off not going down that particular road together again."

The man must have been a good lawyer. He said it with such confidence that I had to wonder if he'd rehearsed it in front of the mirror a time or two the moment he knew Lily was dead.

"Funny. That's not what we heard at all. Lily tried to dump you, but you weren't interested. She was afraid for her life, Counselor."

He didn't flinch, not even bat an eye. He did clench his fists together on his desktop for a split second, and I could see a hint of anger flash through his eyes. We were getting to him, but he was keeping his temper in check.

At least for the moment.

"You're mistaken," he answered icily after three full seconds.

"So then you deny meeting her in April Springs less than an hour before she was murdered?" Phillip asked. The tone and texture of his question were pure cop, and it was clear that the attorney knew it.

"I'm sorry, but you two failed to introduce yourself beyond your names. In what capacity are you here asking me about a former relationship of mine that is none of your business?"

"I used to be the chief of police in April Springs," Phillip said.

"The key phrase being 'used to be.' And you?" he asked as he turned to me.

I wasn't about to confess that I was a donutmaker by trade, not that there was anything wrong with what I did for a living. Shoot, there were times I even considered it a noble profession, but I knew it would just open me up for derision if I admitted it now. "I'm a concerned citizen," I said.

He wanted to throw us out on the spot; I could see it in his expression and his posture, but he managed to subjugate it. "I'm afraid we have nothing more to discuss, then."

"Does that mean that you're denying that you met with Lily Hamilton in April Springs last night before she was murdered?"

He didn't even bother answering. "Good day," was all that he'd say.

We were back out in my Jeep when I said, "I should have known that a lawyer would be too guarded to admit to anything."

"Suzanne, it was worth a try, no matter what the outcome," Phillip said. "Besides, don't be so sure that this visit was pointless."

"What do you mean?"

"We've let him know that someone is claiming that they saw him with Lily the night she was murdered."

"But no one named him specifically," I reminded my stepfather.

"Maybe not, but Kinder doesn't know that. Besides, he fits the bill as the 'mysterious stranger' perfectly."

"I agree, but a little proof would be nice," I said.

"We'll keep digging into it," Phillip said, "but I wanted to see how he'd react. That man has a temper, no matter how well he was able to keep it in check. It was pretty clear that he wanted to punch me in the mouth and throw us out of his office, in that order."

"Then you don't believe his story, either," I said.

"That they decided together not to see each other anymore? Not a chance," Phillip said. "Now we just have to find a way to prove that he was in April Springs last night after all."

I thought about that. "We don't exactly have the resources to compel him to tell us anything, or make him provide us with an alibi," I said.

"We might not be able to apply direct pressure, but we know people who can," Phillip said as he reached for his cell phone.

I put a hand on his before he could call out. "We can't do that, though."

"Suzanne, part of being a past police chief is that other folks in law enforcement take my calls. Why shouldn't we use every resource we have at our disposal?"

"Jake and Chief Grant need to do their jobs, and we need to do ours," I said a little more strongly than I probably should have.

"We're the amateurs, is that it?"

"I know sometimes that it's a hard pill to swallow, but that about sums it up. We can dig around the edges and interview our suspects within reason, but we can't use coercion to force them to speak with us."

"You're right," he said as he put his phone away. "Sorry. I forgot my place in the food chain for a second there."

I laughed. "You've really changed over the years, haven't you?"

He looked at me to see if I was making fun of him, but when he saw my affection for him in my expression, he eased up immediately. "I blame your mother."

"I do too, for so many reasons," I said with a smile. "She has a way of influencing those around her, doesn't she?"

"I'm not saying that it's necessarily a bad thing, but she's definitely softened me around the edges."

"That's a nice way of putting it. Momma is a force of nature."

"She is that," he said. "Speaking of your mother, shouldn't we have heard from her about now?"

At that moment my cell phone rang. "How cool would it be if that was her now?"

"It would be crazy," he said.

I looked at the screen. "Then crazy things are happening, because it's her."

"Speak of the devil, and she appears," I said in lieu of my more standard greeting.

"Suzanne, have you been drinking?" Momma asked me after a second or two of hesitation.

"Nothing stronger than Trish's sweet tea," I admitted. "Your husband and I were just wondering when we'd hear from you, and the next thing we know, you're calling. I hope you have some news for us, because we're not doing so great on our own."

"I have achieved mixed results so far," she admitted. "Are you driving and talking to me at the same time? If you are, please pull over. I'm always concerned something will happen when you're distracted."

"Momma, I'm in a *constant* state of distraction. Talking to you isn't going to make me any safer on the road, I can promise you that."

"We're parked, Dot," Phillip interjected.

"Spoilsport," I said as I stuck my tongue out at him.

He just shrugged, but I could see that he was smiling.

"Are you talking to me still?" Momma asked.

"No, that was a sidebar. Sorry. How has your search been going?"

"I found the mystery man in Lily's life, if that helps," Momma said.

"Do you mean Franklin Kinder?" I asked.

"I see you two haven't been idle," she said, clearly a little put off that we'd already tracked the attorney down.

"For all the good it did us. We just left him in his office in Union Square," I said.

"I hope you didn't aggravate him. He's reputed to have quite a temper," Momma warned.

"I pushed him a bit," Phillip said, "but he kept it under control."

"Phillip Martin, need I remind you that you are no longer the chief of police of April Springs, or anywhere else for that matter?" Momma asked him pointedly.

"There's no need. Suzanne already did that for you," he said with a hint of hurt in his voice. I suddenly felt bad for bringing him in check, but it had needed to be said, and I'd said it.

"It wasn't anything that blunt," I said. "Momma, we *had* to push him a little."

"That's debatable, but since you did, what did you discover?" she asked.

"That his reputation for being a hothead is probably richly deserved," Phillip said.

"I thought you said that he kept his temper in check?"

"He did, but that doesn't mean that he didn't want to...be a bit more aggressive."

More likely he wanted to take a swing at Phillip, but I didn't blame him for downplaying it. After all, we didn't want Momma feeling as though we were taking unnecessary chances. My goodness. When we were investigating a violent murder, it was impossible to keep ourselves a hundred percent safe. All we could do was try to manage the risk as best we could, and I felt as though we'd done that, at least so far.

"We didn't learn anything other than he is excellent at stonewalling," I confessed. "Do you have anything else for us?"

"I've also been looking into this business mystery. There may be something to it after all," she said.

"What do you mean?" I asked.

"Lily wasn't nearly as wealthy as she led people to believe," Momma said. "In fact, she somehow managed to burn through her inheritance at a substantial pace. The truth of the matter is that I was shocked to discover that she was deeply in debt when she died. Her finances were a house of cards, susceptible to collapsing in the lightest breeze."

"So she might have been willing to peddle her influence for money after all," I said.

"How deeply in debt was she?" Phillip asked.

"Deeper than any sane person should be," Momma replied. "It wouldn't surprise me to hear that she borrowed money from some unorthodox people. I imagine Lily was too prideful to let anyone know how she'd gotten herself into such a bind."

"How did it happen?" I asked. "Do you have a clue as to how things got that dire?"

"From what I've been able to gather, she used her substantial inheritance, plus more, to curry favor with the people she wanted to accept her. Evidently the cost to be the queen of clubs was more than she could afford."

I liked that. The Queen of Clubs. It was nice phrasing. Maybe Momma should have been a writer. No, she was too successful as a businesswoman. According to my one-time bookclub friend, 'writing' and 'money' didn't usually go hand in hand, unless the words 'doesn't make' go with them.

"Then if she owed the wrong people, they could have demanded satisfaction in the form of favors, just like Ray Blake implied," Phillip said.

"It's a possibility," Momma admitted, "but I don't want you two digging around in whatever passes for organized crime in our part of the world, and I mean it."

"Relax, Momma," I said. "It's beyond our scope and our ability." I looked over at Phillip. "Right, Phillip?"

"Right," he said, though clearly he wasn't happy about it.

"I'm sure that leaves you with plenty of other people to suspect," Momma said. "Who else is on your list?"

"At the moment, it's pretty crowded. We've got Nathan Billings, Travis Johnson, Mercy Host, Jessie Carlton, and Franklin Kinder, though the last one is probably going to be a wash. We need some kind of leverage on him to get him to talk to us, but I don't know where we can get it."

"I may know someone who could help you," Momma admitted reluctantly.

When no names were forthcoming, I asked, "Care to share a name with us?"

"No, at least not until I've checked to be sure that it's agreeable for my source to speak with you," she said cagily.

"Come on, Momma. Throw us a bone here."

"Suzanne, there are clearly a great many people you can speak with even if Kinder doesn't work out. Please be careful, will you both promise me? You're my two favorite people on this earth, and I'd hate for anything to happen to either one of you."

"Sure, but you love *me* more, right?" I asked with a laugh.

Phillip shook his head, but he was hiding a smile as well.

"I'm sorry, I didn't hear the question. You're breaking up. I've got to go."

"She's cagy, isn't she?" I asked Phillip after the phone call ended.

"It's one of the many things I love about her," he said.

"Me too," I agreed. "Since Union Square seems to be a bust, we should probably head back to April Springs."

As I started to drive, he said, "You sound reluctant to go."

"It's just that I hate being this close to Napoli's without getting something to eat," I admitted.

"We just had big lunches, though," Phillip pointed out.

"Sure, but come on. It's Napoli's."

He smiled. "We'd better not."

"I know, but I can still feel a bit wistful about it, can't I?" I asked as I drove by the DeAngelis restaurant and headed back to April Springs.

I just hoped my stomach found a way to forgive me for not stopping.

Chapter 11

"SHOULD WE USE THE DRIVE back productively to try to figure out where we stand?" Phillip asked me as I headed back home.

"We might as well," I said. "Let's list our suspects first."

"Ours? Or the case's?" he asked me.

"Everybody, including the folks we can't investigate ourselves," I said.

"Okay, then that means we've got Jessie Carlton, Mercy Host, Nathan Billings, and Travis Johnson," he said.

"And we can't forget Ally Tucker and Franklin Kinder, either," I added.

"Maybe the Mob connection isn't so far-fetched after all given what your mother was able to uncover, even though we don't have a name or a face to go with it."

"Or do we?" I asked as a sudden hunch hit me.

"What do you mean?"

"What if one of our suspects is *in* the Mob, or at least representing what goes for a crime empire in our parts?" I asked.

"I guess anything is possible at this point," Phillip said. "Do you have any likely candidates in mind?"

"As a matter of fact, I do. Didn't it seem odd to you that Franklin Kinder didn't have any clients or staff? What if he's just acting as a front for someone or something else?"

"We should get someone to check that out," Phillip said, and then he hastily added, "I don't mean us, but someone."

"Why don't you call Chief Grant and run it past him? Just because Jake and I have a wall between us when it comes to this investigation doesn't mean that you have to participate."

"I'll call him, but not just yet," he said. "It could be someone else, after all."

"Meaning?"

"I never cared for Ally Tucker. What if she's into more than we realize? She seems to have a pretty lavish lifestyle."

"I understand a good realtor can make some serious money," I said.

"So can someone in the Mob's pocket," he said.

"We might as well put Nathan and Travis on the potential rat list too while we're at it. And let's not forget Mercy or Jessie. They have organized crime written all over them."

"You're joking, but I've seen some odder things in my life," he said.

"I don't see how we can ask Chief Grant to look into every last one of our suspects for a criminal tie-in," I said.

"Maybe we'll hold off on that angle until we have something more solid. How about this mystery business connection? And what about the mystery man she was meeting right before she was murdered? Could they be one and the same?"

"Did Lily seem like the type to mix business and pleasure to you?" I asked him.

"Honestly, I didn't really know her all that well. We'd share hellos at the bank or the post office, but that was about it. What about you? Was she a fan of your donuts?"

"If she was, she did a remarkable job of keeping it to herself," I said. "I'm willing to wager that she didn't step foot into Donut Hearts more than half a dozen times since I started running the place, and those were mainly to supply meetings she wanted to treat."

"You and I may have run in different circles, but Dot didn't. I wonder if she'll get permission to share that name with us?"

"We'll just have to wait until she tells us," I said as he pulled out his cell phone. "Phillip, tell me you're not calling Momma and asking her so soon."

"Hey, I can ring up my wife whenever the mood hits me," he said with a smile.

"She's going to think we're pushing her," I warned him.

"I'll risk it," he said.

When Momma picked up, Phillip said, "Dot, Suzanne and I are on our way back to April Springs, and you'd be so proud of us."

"No doubt, but is there any reason in particular?"

"We drove right past Napoli's, and we didn't stop in to grab a bite to eat," he boasted.

"I'm not sure that calls for praise," she said. "The DeAngelis women are wonderful chefs and excellent company in general. Actually, I was just getting ready to call you."

"Is it about that name you were going to give us?" I asked her.

"Yes. I spoke with my source, and they refuse to allow me to share their name with you," she said.

"I notice you were gender neutral when you answered that question," I said.

"That's very astute of you, Suzanne."

"How about the rest of it?" Phillip prodded.

"Are you looking over my shoulder impatiently, dear?" she asked him softly. It was full of dire warning, and I was pleased to see that Phillip got the message loud and clear.

"Nothing of the sort," he said quickly. "I just missed the sound of your voice." From anybody else, it would have sounded lame, but Phillip actually made the words sincere, and I didn't doubt that the sentiment was true.

"You are a sweet man," she said. "Good-bye for now."

"Bye," he said.

When he glanced over at me, I said, "Note that I'm foregoing the perfect opportunity to say 'I told you so,'" I told him with a slight smile.

"We got something, anyway," he replied.

"A negative response," I corrected him.

"But a response nonetheless. So, let's get back to our analysis of the case."

I thought about it for a few moments before I spoke. "How about motive? Jealousy could go for Jessie and Mercy."

"And a different type for Franklin," he interjected.

"True. Let's see. Under Greed, we've got some multiples in the ladies, as well as our mystery businessman," I added. "I'm not quite sure what word describes Nathan and Travis. Is it just me, or are they rather strange bedfellows in all of this?"

"Travis wants to be mayor, but I don't think he'd kill to get the job," Phillip said.

"Maybe not as a calculated move, but he could have killed her if she goaded him. Nathan is a bit of a puzzle, though."

"He doesn't seem all that impartial, does he?" Phillip asked.

"Maybe he's just trying to do a hard job under difficult circumstances and alienating too many folks along the way," I pointed out.

"It's possible," my stepfather said after a few moments of thought. "I never would have believed that so many people would have a reason to want to see Lily Hamilton dead."

"Isn't that the way of it?" I asked. "This isn't the first time I've been amazed by my suspect list. I can't quit thinking about the fact that Lily was broke when she died. How can that fact *not* be related to her murder?"

"I wish we could find out who was set to inherit her estate, that is if there had even been one," Phillip said. "I doubt an attorney is going to just provide us with that information."

"We may have to wait until her estate goes into probate," I agreed, "but if there's nothing there but debts, I doubt anyone is going to be in any hurry to get that particular party started." I drove a bit more before I asked, "Does it sound as though Lily had *any* assets at all when she died?"

"Not that I'm aware of," my stepfather said.

"What about life insurance?" I asked. "If one of our suspects was named as her beneficiary, that would give them a financial motive to want to see her dead."

"Sure, but insurance agents are just about as cagy as attorneys are," Phillip said, "particularly when they might have to pay out a big policy. Did Lily have any family?"

"Not that I know of," I said. "Then again, she could have left it to the Flat Earth Society for all we know, and that's assuming that she even had a policy. It's probably just another dead end, at least as far as we'll be able to investigate."

As we neared the town limits sign to April Springs, Phillip said, "Well, that was a colossal waste of time. I don't know about you, but I'm more confused than I was when we left Union Square."

"I wish I could say that I wasn't, but I can't," I said.

"Then what should we do?"

"If it's all the same to you, I'd like to take another run at Nathan Billings. He's a bit of a wild card in all of this, and I think we should try to get to the bottom of what he's really after."

"Sounds good to me," Phillip said. "When you can't see any light at all, one direction is just as good as another."

"I'm not sure that's true under any circumstances, but I get your drift," I said.

I parked my Jeep in front of City Hall, but when we got to Nathan Billings's office, we had a surprise waiting for us.

Our mayor, at least for the moment, was there, and he was clearly upset about something.

"George, is everything okay?" I asked him as we approached the two men.

"Everything is fine, except for the fact that this lightweight is trying to give my job away," George said angrily.

"I told you before, I don't appreciate you calling me names," Nathan said defiantly, but it was clear that he was a little bit cowed by the mayor's aggressive behavior. George was looming over the man, and his face was red, his fists clenched.

"Then stop trying to weasel your buddy's way into *my* job," George said.

Phillip stepped up. "Everybody needs to take a deep breath and calm down."

"I'm as calm as I'm going to get. You two are the ones who alerted me to what was going on. You were both right. It is a coup," George said angrily.

I touched his arm lightly. "Take it easy, Mr. Mayor."

"Who knows how long I'll have that title, thanks to this guy."

"I didn't think you even wanted the job," Nathan pointed out.

"It's mine to give up, not yours to take away!"

I hadn't seen George that angry in years, and if I were being honest about it, it made me happy. Not because his blood pressure was probably through the roof but because he was fighting back and not just rolling over and taking it.

"The bylaws clearly state..." Nathan started to say when he was again interrupted.

"You can take your bylaws and...stuff them," George finished. There was no doubt in my mind that he'd been planning a more colorful command, but he managed to hold back as he turned and stormed out of the office.

Once he was gone, Nathan turned to us, clearly seeking sympathy. "I don't know why the man is so upset. I'm just following the procedures that were laid out long before I ever took office."

"What's going to happen?" Phillip asked him.

"Whether the mayor likes it or not, in twenty-four hours, the head of the town council will assume the duties of mayor until a special election can be held no later than six months after he is sworn in."

"So, your buddy gets the job that he's been craving for years," I said, feeling some of George's anger. "Everybody in town knows that you are in Travis Johnson's pocket."

"I won't take that from the outgoing mayor, and I won't take it from you, young lady!" he snapped at me.

I was about to reply when Phillip stepped forward. "I'll tell you this once. Watch your tone when you speak to her, or you're going to regret it."

Was my stepfather actually defending my honor? As sweet as the sentiment was, I was entirely capable of doing that for myself. "I've got this, Phillip," I said as I put a hand on his arm and smiled gently.

When I turned to the head of the Board of Elections, my smile was gone. "Nathan, you can posture and protest all you want, but if you go through with this, you're not going to last a month in this town," I said.

"Is that a threat?" he asked as he glanced over at Phillip, who was clearly none too happy with him at the moment.

"I'd say that it's more like a look into your future," I said. "It won't be because of me, but everyone will know what you did and why."

Nathan looked at me icily, and then without another word, he walked out of his own office.

"Is it me, or do people keep on walking out on us?" I asked Phillip.

"Maybe it's our winning personalities," he said with a smile.

"About earlier," I said.

Before I could explain, he jumped in. "Suzanne, I'm sorry. I just couldn't stand idly by and watch him try to browbeat you. I'm old-fashioned that way, but I know you can fight your own battles fine without me. I apologize."

It was something for him to say that, and I was touched again. "I was just going to say thank you."

"Liar," he said with a grin.

"True enough," I countered with a smile of my own.

"Do you think Nathan will really do what he's threatening?" Phillip asked me.

"I'm afraid so. If George gets ousted, we'll never get him to run again, let alone serve as mayor, and I for one don't think this town can afford to go forward without him."

"I agree, but that kind of puts us on a tight deadline, doesn't it?"

"That's okay. I work well under pressure. How about you?"

"I didn't used to, but I've gotten better at it," he said with a grin. "So, what now?"

"Let's go talk to Travis Johnson."

"What can he tell us?" Phillip asked me as we headed out of City Hall.

"I want to know about his real relationship with Lily, and I also want to know if he's behind this push to get into office or if it's Nathan Billings's idea."

"That thought never even occurred to me," Phillip said. "Do you have a reason for believing that Travis is being pushed into the job?"

"I have no idea, but there's only one way to find out."

"*If* he'll tell us the truth," Phillip countered.

"There's always that, but even if he lies, that will tell us something, too."

Chapter 12

"TRAVIS, DO YOU HAVE a second?" I asked him as we walked into the third of his dry-cleaner shops we'd visited in the area. We'd had to go all the way to Maple Hollow to find him. "I didn't know you worked behind the counter at your shops."

"I had to fire the manager here yesterday," he said gruffly. "She was stealing from me, and I won't stand for that."

"Kind of like the way that you're stealing the mayor's job?" I asked him.

Travis waved a hand in the air. "That's never going to happen, and we all know it."

To say the least, I was surprised by his statement. "When was the last time you spoke with Nathan Billings?"

"First thing this morning," he said gruffly. "I told him to drop it."

"Why would you do that?" Phillip asked.

"I don't want the job that way," he said. "Nobody's going to respect me for booting George out and taking his place on a technicality. Don't get me wrong. I can't stand the man, but the people of April Springs keep electing him, at least they did until this last election, and I'm not going to go against their wishes."

"That's awfully magnanimous of you, given how you've felt in the past," I said.

"Let's just say that I've had a taste of what I'd be in for, and I'm not interested in the job anymore," he said.

"Has someone been putting pressure on you already before you're even in office?" Phillip asked him pointedly. "You can talk to us."

"That's probably exactly what I shouldn't be doing, but I won't be bullied, no matter who is doing it," he said defiantly.

"Who's been trying to bully you? Nathan?" It was hard to imagine the head of the Board of Elections making Travis Johnson do anything he didn't want to do.

"*Him*? Hardly. I can handle him," he said derisively. "No, someone else implied that as soon as I got the job, they were going to expect certain things from me that I'm not willing to deliver."

"Who approached you?" I asked.

"That I won't say," he said. "We use a lot of chemicals in my business, and most of them are highly flammable. I can't afford any 'accidents' around here, if you know what I'm saying. It's all a bit too melodramatic for my taste anyway. Who knew there were thugs working behind the scenes in April Springs?"

"Tampering with an elected official is a felony," Phillip said. "There are laws to protect you."

"That's the thing, though. I wasn't elected. I'll keep my spot on the council, but George Morris is welcome to that job."

"Then maybe you'd better tell Nathan that, because he's planning on swearing you in tomorrow as our next mayor."

"What? That's insane. After what I told him earlier? Where did you hear that?"

"From his own lips not an hour ago," I said.

"Excuse me. I've got a phone call to make," he said as he walked into the back of his dry cleaner's.

After a minute, Phillip asked me, "Should we wait for him?"

"I don't think he's going to tell us anything else," I said. "Let's go back to April Springs. Is that okay with you?"

"Like I said before, I'm following your lead."

As we drove, Phillip said, "I can't imagine anyone threatening to burn his businesses down if he doesn't do what he's told. I didn't think April Springs was that kind of town. It didn't used to be, at least not on my watch."

"You're not blaming Stephen Grant, are you?" I asked him sharply.

"No! Of course not. I'm just saying that the world's changed, and not necessarily for the better."

I shrugged. "Parts of it maybe, but if change didn't happen, you wouldn't be with Momma," I reminded him.

"That's a fair point. Evidently whoever Lily had a deal with has come after Travis to honor it. Why would they do that?"

"Maybe they've set things in motion that they can't stop," I said. "Substituting one mayor for another may be their only option."

"Does that mean that they tried to strong-arm George, too?" Phillip asked me.

"We can ask him, but I can't see anyone trying to get George Morris to do *anything* he doesn't want to do, can you?"

"Not a chance," Phillip said. "But if Travis isn't interested in the job and Nathan keeps pushing him, maybe someone's gotten to Nathan Billings."

"If they did, I can't imagine him being that tough a nut to crack," I said. "Let's go see if he's back in his office the second we get into town."

The head of the Board of Elections wasn't there, though. From the look of things, when he'd walked out during our conversation, he hadn't come back.

"What do we do now?"

"We call George. I want to see if anyone has approached him, just in case," I said as I pulled out my cell phone and made the call. It was a short one. Not only had the mayor never been approached about doing something shady, but he didn't believe that anyone would try to get Lily Hamilton to do anything either. I didn't have the heart, or the need at the moment, to tell him about Lily's financial woes.

"Well, that's another dead end," I said after I hung up. I'd put my phone on speaker, but Phillip had remained silent the entire time.

"Where do we go now?"

"Well, at least we have other viable suspects to speak with," I said.

"I'd still like to know what Mercy was looking for, and I'm curious about Jessie's, Ally's, and Franklin's alibis."

"So we keep poking and prodding until something breaks our way," Phillip said in agreement.

"We really don't have much choice. You know what? Let's leave Franklin alone for now. I want to pursue some other angles before we take another swing at him, and I'd love to have more information than we do now."

"Don't you mean ammo?" Phillip asked me with a smile.

"In this business, isn't it the same thing?"

"I wonder if Stephen Grant and Jake are having any more luck than we are?" he asked.

"We can't call them, Phillip," I said sternly.

"I know, I know," he answered. I wasn't sure if he'd been hoping that I'd change my mind, but he should have known me better.

A deal was a deal.

We were going to have to figure this out on our own, or someone else was going to have to solve Lily Hamilton's murder.

Those were our only options, at least as far as I was concerned.

"Seriously? Why are you two here?" Jessie asked us the moment she answered her door.

"We never got a chance to finish talking with you earlier," I said. "I can see that the wake is over, since there isn't anybody here."

"That's not entirely true," she said. "Gabby Williams is helping me clean up."

I stepped inside as I said, "Really? Gabby's here? I'd love to help. Think of it as my way of paying my respects."

Jessie wanted to throw us out—I could see it in her glare—but her manners got the better of her, and by the time she'd been able to override her upbringing, I was already walking into the kitchen.

"Suzanne, Phillip. What are you two doing here?" Gabby asked as we joined her.

"Why does everybody keep asking us that?" I asked as I started grabbing dishes and carrying them to the sink. "We all pay our respects in different ways."

"I tried to tell them that we had this under control," Jessie said.

Gabby shook her head. "Nonsense. If they want to help, they should be able to. Phillip, would you mind carrying those large trash bags outside and then putting them at the curb? Tomorrow's pickup day, and I'd hate for there to be a reminder sitting there all week for Jessie. Show him how you'd like them arranged, Jessie. We both know how meticulous you are about your waste."

"Come on, Phillip," she said, resigning herself to the fact that we were going to help whether she liked it or not.

Once they were gone, I asked, "What do you want to talk to me about alone?"

"How did you know?" Gabby asked me.

"We've known each other too long, Gabby. What's up?"

"I just heard from Lily's insurance agency. She named me the sole beneficiary for her life insurance policy."

"That's amazing," I said. "You said you were her best friend. I'm so glad she thought of you that way as well."

"So am I," she said. "Do I have to use the money to pay off her bills, or do I get it all?"

"I have no idea," I answered honestly.

"I'll have to find an attorney and ask them," she said. "We can't seem to keep good ones here in April Springs."

"To be fair, some of them didn't leave voluntarily," I replied, remembering a local murdered attorney case I'd managed to solve, with some help from my friends, of course.

"At any rate, it's the thought that counts," Gabby said.

"Why is it a secret?" I asked her before Jessie and Phillip could return.

"I don't want Jessie to know unless I have to tell her. She thinks *she* was Lily's best friend. When she brought up throwing this wake, I wasn't in any position to refuse, but Lily made sure that I knew *exactly* where I rated in her book, and that's all that matters to me. The money is almost a side issue."

"But it's still an important one," I said. "You don't want to spend that money and then find out that you owe the estate a whopping sum."

"Suzanne, you know me to be a prudent businesswoman. I'll investigate it before I do anything, but I wanted to share the news with you. I shouldn't have to say this, but I'd appreciate it if you didn't breathe a word of this to anyone else."

"I'm honored that you trusted me with it," I said sincerely.

"I just had to tell someone," she answered.

It wasn't exactly a ringing endorsement, but it still said volumes that Gabby trusted me. We'd come a long way since my first day at the donut shop, when she'd told me point blank that she'd expected me to be out of business in six months.

I'd been so happy to prove her wrong, but things had gotten tight on occasion, and even after all of these years, I still wasn't out of the woods yet as far as considering myself a roaring success.

When Jessie and Phillip returned, Gabby washed her hands as she said, "Jessie, since you have more than enough help now, there's something I need to see about immediately."

Jessie looked distressed that Gabby was leaving her alone with us, but I knew what she was going to do. The second she was out the door, she was going to start looking for attorneys to see just what a windfall she'd really gotten from her late friend.

"There's no reason for you two to stay," Jessie said. "I can handle it from here."

"Nonsense," I said. "Did you have a good turnout for the memorial?" I asked as I kept working. I knew that it would be harder for her to throw us out if we were actually doing something.

"It was an amazing tribute to how many folks loved Lily," she said. Quite a few had hated her as well, but I didn't feel right bringing that up. I was about to respond when Phillip's phone went off, a train whistle that never failed to catch me by surprise. "Sorry, I've got to take this," he said as he stepped outside. I was hoping it was Momma with some good news. We could use it.

"I'm sure you all told stories about Lily," I said. "I know one thing I always remember when a friend passes away is where I was at the time it happened and what I was doing."

"There were some of those," Jessie admitted.

"Did you share?" I asked. It was a subtle way of asking her for an alibi, something I'd done in the past. I wasn't particularly proud of intruding on someone's grief, but then again, in my mind, I was doing the ultimate service to the victim by trying to catch their killer, so in this case, at least in my mind, the end justified the means.

"It was too personal to share with the others," she said guiltily.

"You can tell me," I suggested softly. "It will do you good to say it out loud." I didn't know if it would or not, but I really wanted to know.

After a great deal of hesitation, she finally admitted, "I was with Travis Johnson," and I felt my interest suddenly piqued.

"What were you doing with Travis?" I asked.

"Don't make me say it out loud," she said as her face started to redden. "We got close during the campaign, and we felt it all coming to an end with the election results coming in. The truth of the matter is that we slipped away to the supply closet the moment Lily stepped outside, and er, we spent some time together there, alone."

"When did you come back out?"

"That's what's been wracking me with guilt. Travis and I have figured out that while Lily was being murdered with that infernal ballot box, we were canoodling in the closet. We heard George make the announcement, and we were both stunned by the news. If only I'd been with her, maybe I could have stopped it from happening."

"You have no way of knowing that," I said, doing my best to comfort her. "Besides, even if you'd been right by her side, all that means is that there may have been two murders instead of one."

"I never thought about it that way," she said with a sliver of hope in her voice. "Do you honestly think it's possible?"

"Not only possible, but likely," I said, even though I had no idea if that were true or not. All I did know was that Travis and Jessie now both had alibis for the murder. I knew how embarrassed Jessie had been to admit what she'd been doing, and I realized that there was no way she would have told me if it was a lie, even to save her own skin. As a matter of fact, it was growing pretty clear that she regretted opening up to me in the first place. What can I say? I'm a good listener. It's my number-one skill when it comes to investigating murder.

"Suzanne, you can't tell a soul what I just told you," she said desperately.

"Unless I'm under oath in a court of law, your secret is safe with me, Jessie, but what's the issue? You and Travis are both single adults. There's no crime in finding a little romance wherever you can."

"The problem is that Travis has a girlfriend," she told me. "He made me swear not to tell anyone what we'd been doing, but I couldn't keep it in."

"Your secret is safe with me," I said as Phillip came in after knocking on the doorframe.

"Suzanne, there's something we need to take care of as soon as possible, if Jessie can really do without us here."

Our reluctant host nodded in agreement, clearly eager to get rid of us both but me especially. "Please, feel free to go. I have this."

"If you're sure," I said. I hated making her feel suddenly so uncomfortable around me, but I hadn't forced her to talk to me, and I certainly hadn't compelled her to tell me about her secret tryst.

"I'm positive," she said as she walked us out. As Phillip and I turned to go, she motioned to me with a finger to her lips.

I nodded, took out a pretend key, and locked my mouth, throwing away the key after I was finished with it.

The look of relief on her face was clear, and I'd do my best to keep my word.

Before Phillip could tell me about his phone call, I said, "Jessie and Travis are in the clear unless we hear something otherwise."

"What did she tell you?"

"It's confidential, so I need you to trust me on it," I said. "I gave her my word, and I don't want to break it, especially not three minutes after I offered it."

"If you're satisfied, then so am I," he said. "In a way, I'm kind of relieved. We still have way too many people on our list as it is to suit me."

"What was that call about? Was it Momma?"

"It was," he agreed. "Evidently she's got some interesting information to share with us, but she didn't want to do it over the phone."

"I suppose there's time to run by your place before I head back to the cottage," I said. "It's getting close to dinnertime, and my stomach's already rumbling."

"Are you meeting Jake to eat?" he asked me as we got into the Jeep.

"No, I'm on my own tonight. He'll be dining at his temporary desk at the station, I'm sure."

"Then you should eat with us. Dot made a pot roast, and there's always more than we can handle for a week."

"Sounds good," I said, giving in instantly.

"You're not even going to fight me on it?" Phillip asked with a grin.

"Not when it comes to Momma's pot roast, I'm not," I said as I started driving there.

"You are a woman after my own heart," he answered.

As I drove to Momma and Phillip's place, I couldn't help wondering what she'd been able to uncover.

With any luck, we might just be able to eliminate another suspect or two.

That, along with getting pot roast for dinner, made this a pretty good evening, and if she'd made dessert as well, which I was sure she had, it was going to be a smashing success.

It was not to be though, at least not immediately.

My cell phone rang, and there was no way that I wasn't going to take that particular call.

Chapter 13

"HEY, STRANGER," I SAID as I answered Jake's call. I'd pulled over first, since he wasn't thrilled with me talking while I was driving any more than Momma was.

"Suzanne, I need to see you at the cottage as soon as you can make it here. I hope you're in town." There was no playfulness in his voice, and I had to wonder what had happened.

"Are you okay?"

"I'm fine. How soon can you make it?"

"Let me drop Phillip off at his place, and then I'll be right there. Ten minutes?"

"Five would be better," he said, "but don't speed on my account."

"I'll do my best. Can I at least get a hint as to what this is about?"

"I'll see you soon," he said, ignoring my request as he hung up.

"What was that all about?" Phillip asked me.

"There's been a change of plans. I'm going to drop you off and then go see Jake at the cottage. I'm not sure how long it's going to take, so I may have to take a pass on dinner."

He knew better than to ask me if something was wrong. "Tell you what. It's not all that far. I'll walk home."

As he opened his car door, I said, "You don't have to do that."

"It's okay. I need the exercise," he said with a grin as he continued. "I've got pot roast waiting on me, so it's not going to hurt to work up an appetite. Tell you what. If you can still make it, come over after you and Jake have talked. Better yet, bring him with you."

"We'll see," I said.

"I get it," he answered, and then he shut his door.

I got moving. Now I'd make it in less than five minutes, but it was still five minutes too long for me.

I couldn't wait to hear what Jake had to say.

"How many laws did you break getting here?" my husband asked me after giving me a brief hug.

"None that I know of. Phillip decided to walk home. What's going on?"

"Take this dollar," he said as he offered me a single bill.

"You nearly gave me a heart attack getting me over here so you could give me a *dollar*?" I asked him. "Please tell me there's more to this than that, Jake."

He continued to hold out the money without comment. I took it from him, folded it up, and then shoved it into my pants pocket.

"Thanks, I guess."

"You're welcome," he said as he took out the small notebook he was never without and wrote something in it.

After he tore off the top sheet and handed it to me, I read, "*In consideration of one dollar, I hereby retain Suzanne Hart's services for the next seven days.*"

"So, I'm working for you now?" I asked him with a puzzled grin.

"You're on retainer. I'm hiring you as a consultant," he said.

"Don't tell me you've suddenly developed an interest in making donuts. This is about Lily, isn't it?"

"Of course it is. I've been going round and round with Stephen Grant about how he's wasting two precious resources in you and Phillip, but he won't listen."

"So you're skirting his wishes by taking matters into your own hands? That's not like you, Jake."

"I can't help it. If I'd known how this arrangement would make me feel about being muzzled with my own wife, I *never* would have agreed to it in the first place. What do you say?"

"If you're okay with it, then I am, too. I'm afraid I don't have much to share with you, though. Hang on. That's not true. Did you know that Jessie Carlton and Travis Johnson were in the utility closet in the City Hall basement when Lily was murdered? They went in together when she walked outside, and they didn't come back out again until George announced that Lily was dead." Almost as an afterthought, I added, "That was told to me in confidence, so I'd really appreciate if you wouldn't share it with anyone else unless it's absolutely necessary."

"Of course. But do you see what I mean? That's *exactly* what I'm talking about. Travis never would have told the chief that story, or me either for that matter."

"Actually, Jessie told me," I said.

"It doesn't matter. What counts is that you found out valuable information. That wasn't why I called you, though."

"Why *did* you phone? Not that there's a problem with you calling me anytime, day or night."

"You have Franklin Kinder on your list," he said matter-of-factly.

"We do," I said. "As far as I'm concerned, that man is three kinds of shady. He's up to no good, but we weren't able to pin him down on anything."

"He's not a factor in this case," Jake said.

"Why not? What do you know that I don't?"

"Just take my word for it," my husband answered.

"I will, but I thought we were working together?" I asked him. I tried to keep the surprise out of my voice. After all, I'd just told Jake virtually everything Phillip and I had uncovered so far, but he didn't seem all that eager to return the favor. If I didn't know why the attorney was no longer a suspect in his mind, then I couldn't drop him as a suspect.

"He isn't the mysterious stranger you've been looking for," Jake explained. "In fact, he wasn't at City Hall at the time Lily was murdered at all."

"How do you know that?"

"Franklin Kinder was involved in another matter thirty miles away at the time of Lily's death," Jake said. "Please don't ask me for more than that. I probably shouldn't have said that much."

"How sure are you of your information?" I asked him.

"One hundred percent," he said.

"That's all I need then. I'm just as happy he's not a suspect. Phillip and I found it hard to pin the man down about *anything* when we interviewed him."

"Trust me, he's been pinned down quite thoroughly," Jake replied.

"Would you mind sharing with me who else is on your list?"

"Given what you just told me, we're down to three, possibly four suspects, and I'm hoping Momma will help us eliminate another one this evening. How about you?"

"I'll share my list with you first this time," he said, "since you've been doing most of the talking so far. We believe, given the information you've just shared with me, that the killer was either Mercy, Nathan, Ally, or this mystery man she met with before she was murdered."

"So, you believe there really was a mystery man too?" I asked him.

"Witnesses say she met with *someone*, and she was pretty surreptitious about it. Who it might have been I have no idea."

"We don't either, but for what it's worth, our lists match." My cell phone rang, and it was Momma. "Hey. Can I call you right back?"

"Is Jake there with you? You should both come over and have dinner with us. We have some things to talk about."

"Hang on, I'll ask him," I said as I buried my phone in my chest. "Momma wants us to come have pot roast with her and Phillip. Can you squeeze it in?"

He looked so sad when he answered that it was all I could do not to laugh. "Sorry, but I have to get back to the station. We've got something cooking, and I can't miss out on it. It was hard enough to get away for the time I got. Have a bite for me."

"I'll have two, but don't look so glum. If I know Momma, and I do, she'll send me home with an armful of Tupperware for you."

"Dessert too, do you think?" he asked hopefully.

"I'm sure of it," I said.

"I feel a little better about missing the meal then."

I pulled the phone away and spoke. "Jake can't make it, but I'll be there in five minutes," I told her.

"I'm sorry, what were we talking about?" Momma asked. "I was on hold so long that I believe I nodded off for a moment there."

"Ha ha. Very funny. My husband is hoping for some leftovers, and if it's not pushing it, some dessert, too."

"Tell him that he knows that I will take good care of him."

"You always do. I hope you aren't disappointed that it's just me. See you soon," I said.

"Suzanne, I am rarely disappointed in you."

"Not never though, right?" I asked her.

"Child, you are wearing on my last nerve," Momma said. "Goodbye."

"Bye, Momma. See you soon."

After I hung up, Jake said, "Suzanne, thanks for sharing what you've uncovered with me. I hope I don't get you in hot water with Phillip."

I patted the pocket where I'd stashed the bill. "He's just going to be jealous that you didn't hire him, too."

"I figured I was pushing my luck as it was," he said.

"Seriously though, Jake, I don't have to tell anyone about our arrangement," I said. "There's no reason this needs to get out. Nobody needs to know but the two of us."

"I don't know. I feel as though I'm doing something wrong by asking you to hide what we're doing."

"You didn't ask me; I volunteered," I said as I kissed him.

We were interrupted by his cell phone ringing. "Hey, Chief. Yes, I'm on my way. Of course. See you soon." After putting his phone away, Jake said, "The police chief is getting antsy. I'm afraid it's going to be another late night, Suzanne."

"Just be careful," I told him as he kissed me again and then started to go.

"Right back at you," he replied. "Aren't you coming?" he asked as he headed for the door.

"Try to stop me," I said with a grin. "I'm having pot roast, remember?"

"Don't remind me," Jake answered.

We kissed briefly again, and then Jake got into his truck, and I got into my Jeep and started toward Momma's place. I was excited about eating, but if it was possible, I was even more excited about finding out what Momma was going to tell us.

With any luck, it might just help break the case wide open.

"Suzanne, I am always happy to see you. You know that, don't you?" Momma asked as she took my jacket. The days were warming up nicely after a long, wet winter, but with nighttime, sometimes there came a chill that told us all that cold weather wasn't finished with us just quite yet.

"I do," I said. "Why do you ask?"

"Your comment about me being disappointed that Jake couldn't join us bothered me," Momma admitted.

"I'm sorry. I didn't mean for it to be hurtful."

"Then we're good?" she asked me.

"That depends."

"On what?"

"How big a slice of roast I get," I answered with a grin.

"As large as you'd like," she answered with a smile.

"Then we are more than good, we're great!"

"I'm glad. I couldn't bear to be at odds with you," she replied.

"Right back at you. So what's this big news you've got for us?"

"It can wait until we eat," she said. "After all, it's nothing all that pressing."

"Okay, if you say so, but I'd still rather know sooner than later. That way I can focus on the food. You know how distracted I get at times."

"Have you *ever* gotten distracted when it came to food?" Phillip asked with a grin as he walked into the living room where we were still standing.

"That's fair," I said with a smile. "You're right, Momma. Let's eat first and then worry about murder later."

"Thank you, Suzanne."

"Thank you. After all, if you hadn't intervened, I'd probably be eating old donuts for dinner."

"You gave those to Jessie for the wake, remember?" Phillip reminded me.

"I was going more for donuts as a metaphor," I told him.

"That's probably the first time in the history of the world that anyone has ever constructed that particular sentence," Phillip said with a smile.

"Who's hungry?" Momma asked us, clearly happy to have us both there with her.

"I am," Phillip and I said in unison, something that made Momma smile.

"Then let's eat."

I didn't have to be asked twice. I had been smelling that wonderful meal ever since I'd walked in the front door. It was a good thing that no one was between me and the dinner table, or there might have been an accident.

Chapter 14

"HOW DO YOU DO IT, MOMMA?" I asked as I pushed my empty plate away.

"Do what, Suzanne?"

"Produce something that amazing. I can take the exact same ingredients and follow your recipe to a T, but I still can't make a roast as good as you do. Are you holding out on me?"

"What do you mean?" she asked curiously.

"She wants to know if there's a secret ingredient you haven't shared with her," Phillip said, clearly amused by our conversation.

"Of course not," Momma said, acting a bit offended. "I would never do that."

"To anyone, or just to me?" I asked her with a grin.

"Just you," she admitted.

"Well, however you manage it, it was wonderful. Are you sure there's enough left over for me to take Jake some? It's okay if you can't spare it." The truth was that my husband would be heartbroken, but I felt as though I had to at least make the offer.

"I can always make another," she said. "Isn't that right, Phillip?"

"Whatever you say," he answered. "Did I hear there was pineapple upside-down cake for dessert?"

"Do you honestly have room for a treat?" she asked.

"I might take a sliver," he admitted. As she started to cut his portion, he protested, "More than that, Dot."

"That's a sliver," she explained.

"Then I misspoke. I'd like a slab."

She laughed, which was a sound I never grew tired of. "How about a regular serving?"

"That depends. Where does that stand on your scale?"

"Halfway between a sliver and a slab."

"I can get on board with that," he said.

"How about you, Suzanne?"

"The slab sounds good to me," I said, but before she could protest, I amended, "but a regular serving sounds delightful. Jake is going to love you even more than he already does."

"Your husband does an old cook's heart good," Momma said.

After the dessert was finished and the table was cleared, I said, "I hate to even bring this up since our evening has been so delightful, but Momma, you told Phillip you had some information for us."

"I do," she said. "I know who the mysterious stranger was Lily met with soon before she was murdered, and it wasn't what you two thought."

"Does that mean that she *wasn't* meeting a romantic interest?" I asked.

"That is correct. Lily was meeting with the new bank manager about her latest loan application," Momma said.

"At night, and in secret?" I asked incredulously. "Momma, are you sure that someone isn't lying to you?"

"I'm positive," she said. "Evidently Lily came to him for an extension as well as an increase on her personal loan, and she insisted that he tell her the moment he knew."

"Did she get what she was asking for?"

"She did not," Momma said. "It was refused entirely. In fact, I learned that the bank was about to insist on payment in full, regardless of whether Lily won the election or not."

"How did you find all of this out, Dot?" Phillip asked her.

"I have my sources," Momma answered.

"I'm not denying it, but the bank manager himself had to be the one who told you, didn't he? Didn't he break some kind of confidentiality agreement or something?" Phillip asked.

"He is neither an attorney nor a physician," Momma said. "Besides, with Lily dead, he knew that he needed to tell someone so he didn't look like a suspect."

"Why didn't he go straight to Chief Grant?" I asked. If he had, and the chief had told Jake, I would have known about it.

"I advised him to do just that, but he wanted to consult with one of the bank's attorneys first. Unless I miss my guess, Chief Grant is learning about what happened even as we speak."

"I don't suppose it makes any sense that he killed her," I said, mostly musing to myself.

"No, of course not. He had no motive. His predecessor extended the loan originally, and behavior such as that is what caused him to be replaced. The new man seems to have a better grasp of things."

"How do you know him that well already?" Phillip asked his wife.

"We've had occasion to do business together," she admitted. "Naturally when he came to me, I realized exactly what had happened."

"So we can strike him off the list unless we learn something else about the man," I said.

"Does that limit your suspect pool by much?" Momma asked us.

"It helps. We still have Mercy, Nathan, and Ally," I said. "I can feel it in my bones. One of them did it."

"If only that were enough," Phillip said. "Unfortunately, we need proof."

"Don't worry. Tomorrow is another day. We'll get it," I said as I stifled a yawn.

"Suzanne, we're creeping up on your bedtime hour, aren't we?" Momma asked.

"I'm not working at the shop tomorrow," I said. "It's Emma and Sharon's turn. I can stay up a lot longer than I usually do," I added with another yawn.

"Evidently your body doesn't know your work schedule," Momma said. "Let me get Jake's dinner, and you can be on your way. You are stopping your investigation for the night, are you not?"

I looked at Phillip. "If it's all the same to you, I am kind of beat. Would you be okay if we take it back up in the morning?"

"Fine by me," he said.

"Then let's meet for breakfast at the Boxcar Grill, and we can map out our strategy for tomorrow."

"What time is good for you?" he asked.

"Is seven too early?"

"I can be there when Trish opens at six thirty if you'd like," my sleuthing partner said. It was quite a bit different from working with Grace. I usually had to blast her out of bed to get her going in the morning, but Phillip was a kindred early riser.

"Seven will be soon enough," Momma interjected. "Suzanne needs her rest."

"As much as I appreciate the thought, we both know that I'll be up by five at the latest," I said.

"True, but I can hope you'll take advantage of your day off from the donut shop and get some real sleep."

"There will be plenty of time to sleep when I'm dead," I said.

"Suzanne, I've told you before, I detest that expression."

"Sorry," I said as I kissed her cheek. "If it helps, I don't plan on it happening for a very long time, and I expect you to afford me the same courtesy."

"I'll do what I can," she said with a soft smile.

A few minutes later, I left their cottage, carrying containers holding Jake's dinner and dessert, and as I stowed them in the passenger seat of the Jeep, I glanced back inside the cottage I'd just left. Momma and Phillip were having a quiet moment, embracing in the soft light coming from the dining room. At one time, the sight would have made me uneasy, but I had long since come to terms with them being together. It was good and right that Momma had found someone after Dad's death, and while I wouldn't have chosen the former chief of police for her at the time if I'd been given the choice, they continued to work out well together.

Sometimes the second time around was better than the first.

I knew that firsthand because I had Jake to prove it.

When I got home, it was no surprise that my husband wasn't there. Knowing him, he'd be at his temp desk until the wee hours of the night. As much as I wanted to stay up to see him, I knew that I'd fall asleep before he'd even think about making it back home.

Instead, I wrote him a brief but sweet note, and then I took a quick shower and went off to bed. Momma had been right. I knew in my head that my schedule was going to be different tomorrow, but my body was begging for sleep, and I wasn't about to deny it.

Jake was snoring softly beside me when I woke, and instead of getting right up, I lay there and listened to his breathing. He never slept better than when he was working on a case, and I was glad that the chief of police had hired him. I kissed his forehead gently, and then I quietly got dressed and went out into the living room. I had some time before I had to meet Phillip at the Boxcar, but I decided to walk over through the park early so I could spend a little time with Trish first. After Grace, she was one of my dearest friends, and she often protested that I never made enough time for her.

Hopefully this would be a pleasant surprise.

"Your breakfast companion is already waiting on you," Trish said with a laugh as she pointed to Phillip, who was already nursing a cup of coffee at a table in the rear.

"How did you know I was meeting him?" I asked her.

"He couldn't wait to tell me that the two of you were hot on the trail of a killer," Trish said.

"Seriously?" I asked. Was Phillip going around announcing that we were working on Lily's murder together? I loved keeping a low profile—well, as low a profile as I could—so him telling anyone, even Trish, was at odds with that.

"Of course not, you big goof," Trish said. "All he told me was that he was expecting you a bit later. The man didn't say a word about what you were up to."

"Good," I said as I lingered at the front.

"Aren't you going to join him?" Trish asked me.

"In a minute. How have you been?"

"Fine," she said.

"How's the love life?" I asked her. Trish hadn't had much luck in that department lately, and I knew how much she would love to find someone.

"Nonexistent," she said with a grin. "I did have a first date the other night, though."

"Really? Anybody I know?"

"I doubt it. It was with the guy who delivers our supplies."

"How was it?"

"He smelled like mustard," Trish said, making a face.

"I'm sure that was just your imagination," I said.

"No, I'm pretty sure he used it as cologne," Trish countered.

"Even if that were true, which I highly doubt, you can't hold that against him. I smell like donuts all of the time, and we both know it. It doesn't matter how many times I scrub my hide and shampoo my hair, the smell seems to come from my pores."

"Maybe, but who doesn't love the smell of donuts?" she asked me.

"But mustard? Yuck."

"Was that his only crime?" I asked her.

"Well, he kept referring to himself in the third person," she said with a smile.

"Please tell me you're kidding."

"Trish would never do that," she said, this time laughing loudly. "I swear, I kept looking around for somebody named Gregory. It took me ten minutes to remember that was *his* name!"

"So, when's the second date?" I asked her with a wicked grin of my own.

"It's not happening. I'm swearing off men," she said, and then added hastily, "unless I happen to meet a really good one. But until he waltzes through that door with a dozen roses and asks me out on one knee, I'm going to stay single for at least a little while longer."

We both looked at the door as though we were anticipating her Prince Charming arriving. Instead, Larry Jansen walked in, sixty years old, bald, and tipping the scale at near three hundred pounds. It was all Trish and I could do not to burst out laughing, but Larry must have caught something, because he mumbled a hello and then made his way to a table.

"Thanks, Suzanne. I needed a dose of you this morning."

"I feel the same way about you," I said.

Phillip must have noticed that I was already there, because he beckoned me to his table. I made it a point to say hello to Larry as I walked past his table, and soon I found myself at my stepfather's table.

"You're early," I said as I took my seat.

"So are you," he countered. "Don't tell your mother. She thinks I went out for a walk."

"Did you?" I asked him as Trish approached with a cup of coffee and a menu.

"Well, I walked from my truck to the steps, and then I walked up them, past Trish, and all the way to the table. That's a lot of walking if you ask me."

"Is she concerned about you getting enough exercise?" I asked him.

"She's concerned about everything. I've got to have another test this week," he said softly.

I touched his hand lightly. "The cancer isn't back, is it?" He'd gone through a bout of prostate cancer, had surgery to remove it, and had then suffered through a long and slow recovery process.

"That's what the test is going to tell us," he said. "I'm not worried about it, maybe because your mother is worrying enough for both of us." Phillip seemed to shake himself. "Anyway, I don't want to talk about it. After breakfast, who are we going after first?"

"You seem pretty eager to get going," I told him.

"I can't seem to think about much else," he said. "We're close, Suzanne. I'm the one who can feel it now. One or two more little nudges and we're going to catch ourselves a killer today."

"I hope you're right," I said as Trish approached again. "You're eating too, aren't you?"

"Just try to stop me," he said with a smile.

"I wouldn't dare," I replied.

Twenty minutes, later we were finished with our meals, and despite my protests, Phillip grabbed the check before I could get to it.

I looked accusingly at Trish. "You two planned that all along, didn't you?"

"No way," she countered. "I put it halfway between your plates. It's not my fault that you're losing your edge, Suzanne."

"A likely story," I said with a grin. "Thanks for breakfast," I told my stepfather. "Can I at least get the tip?"

"Not today. Maybe next time, though."

"You always say that," I protested.

"Well then, one of these days, I'm going to actually mean it."

After we left, I slid onto the truck's bench seat. It felt odd not driving my Jeep, but it was only right that Phillip got to drive us around today.

I just hoped he was right about his instincts.

I would like nothing better than to nail Lily's killer and hope that life found a way to get back to normal.

Or at least what passed for normal in April Springs.

Chapter 15

"MERCY, WE NEED TO TALK some more," I told one of our final suspects as she answered her door. It was early, and clearly she hadn't been out of bed for long. I didn't understand people who slept in. I thought they were missing the best part of the day, but then again, they all thought I was crazy for getting up before the sun even rose. I was glad that Jake was an early riser, too. I couldn't imagine being married to someone who was sleeping in while I was ready to embrace the day.

"I'm finished speaking with the two of you," she said as she started to close the door.

"If you didn't want to talk to us, then why did you answer the door?" I asked.

"That's none of your business," she said.

"Listen, we're tired of tap-dancing around this. You need to tell us what you were looking for at the crime scene," I pushed. It was getting down to the wire, and the time to tread lightly with our questions was over.

"I won't tell you a thing," she said angrily.

"Was it something that was yours, or Lily's?" I asked her pointedly. "You two had an argument the night she died, didn't you?"

"I don't want to talk about it," Mercy said angrily.

Just then, Belinda Bates, a woman I knew casually, drove up. After she got out of her car, she came running up to us excitedly. "I found it, Mercy!"

"What exactly did you find?" Phillip asked her.

"You're the old chief of police, aren't you?" she asked.

"I prefer to think of it as being retired, not old," Phillip said, clearly a line he'd used before.

"Whatever," Belinda said, dismissing him. "Mercy, I knew that if I went back and retraced your steps I'd find it," she said as she held out a pin. It was an artist's palette, small and gold and shiny.

"*This* is what you were looking for?" I asked her.

"It was my mother's," Mercy said, nearly sobbing as she took the pin from Belinda and caressed it as though it were alive. "It's just about the last thing I ever got from her before she died."

"How did you happen to know that it was missing?" I asked Belinda.

"I was with her when Lily tore it off her and threw it into the bushes," Belinda said.

"Belinda! That's none of their business," Mercy scolded.

"I keep telling you that you have to tell the police. How many times do I have to tell you that, Mercy? Maybe they can talk some sense into you, because I surely haven't had any luck. I was with you after you fought with Lily. I'm your alibi!"

"Then you two did have a fight the night Lily was murdered?" I asked.

"She told me that I'd never get anything higher than second place as long as she was around. I told her that I knew she was in financial trouble and that she shouldn't be so high and mighty much longer," Mercy explained. "Her face went white, and she spotted my pin. She ripped it off my blouse and threw it as hard as she could! I'm not ashamed to admit that I could have killed her at that moment."

"But you didn't," Belinda said quickly. She then turned to Phillip. "I got her out of there, and I took her home with me. We had some tea, calmed down a bit, and then we talked about going back for her pin. I convinced her to wait until morning, but she was obsessed with finding it, so I walked her back over to City Hall. That's when we found out that Lily had been murdered."

"I was there to find my pin, not hide evidence!" she swore. "When I couldn't find it, I figured the police had it, and I'd have to wait to get it back until after whoever killed Lily was caught and tried for the crime. But I didn't kill her!"

"She couldn't have," Belinda said. "She was with me the entire time. When we both left Lily, she was very much alive."

"You'll swear to that in court?" Phillip asked her.

"Why wouldn't I? It's the truth," Belinda said. She then turned back to Mercy. "Let's go tell the real police chief right now. You don't have anything to worry about. I'll be right by your side, Mercy."

"You're a good friend," Mercy said. "Okay. I'm ready."

"Then if you two will excuse us, we need to do this before my friend here changes her mind yet again."

The two women left in Belinda's car, and I turned to Phillip. "Why didn't she tell us that story earlier?"

"Would you, Suzanne? Not only did it cast her in a bad light, but it pointed to her as a prime suspect."

"Not with Belinda backing her up," I said.

"Maybe she didn't think Chief Grant would believe them," Phillip posited.

"What do you think?" I asked him.

"I think she's telling the truth," Phillip admitted. "Mercy isn't our killer."

"Yeah, I agree with you. Man, I kind of wanted her to have done it. Is it wrong to admit that out loud?"

"Not to me," Phillip said, "but I'd probably keep it to myself if I were you. Now we have two viable suspects left. I told you we were getting close."

"It's hard to imagine Ally *or* Nathan as a killer," I said.

"I know, but we both know that it's hard to wrap your head around the fact that just about anybody can be a murderer, given the right circumstances."

"That's true, but what exactly are the right circumstances in this case?" I asked.

"Figuring out the motive is getting tougher and tougher," he said. "Love is out of the picture, unless Nathan and Lily were having a secret affair."

I tried to imagine the two of them together, but I couldn't do it. "No one's whispered a thing about that as even a possibility," I replied. "If Nathan killed her, it has to have something to do with the election."

"Why wouldn't he want Lily to win?" Phillip asked as we got into his truck.

"Could he have ties to the Mob, too?" I asked.

"Why would the Mob be interested in the head of the Board of Elections for our small town?" Phillip asked.

"Beats me," I replied. "How about Ally? Could the bad guys have some kind of leverage on her? They could pressure her to act on their behalf when Lily reneged on her offer. That doesn't make sense either, though."

"Why not?"

"She's five foot nothing," I said. "How could she lift that ballot box above Lily's head? The blow was struck from behind."

"Could Lily have leaned over for something?" Phillip asked.

"It's possible. For that matter, Nathan might have had a problem hitting her from above, too. Lily was a tall woman, and Nathan is barely five foot six."

"I'd love to see the autopsy," Phillip said. "It might give us some insight into the mechanics of the murder."

I thought about asking Jake for it, but Phillip didn't know that we were secretly working together, and I didn't want to put Jake in an awkward position with Chief Grant. I wasn't crazy about keeping information from my investigating partner, but if it meant protecting my husband's reputation, then I'd do it ten out of ten times. "That's not really our bailiwick anyway, is it?" I asked.

"No, I suppose not," he said as he tried to start his truck.

Nothing happened but a series of clicks, though.

"I was afraid of that," he said as he got out his cell phone.

"Is the battery dead?"

"Yeah. I've been meaning to get a new one. This might take a while. I'm going to call Dot and get her to come get us. I can pull the battery and have her take me to the auto supply store to get a new one. Unfortunately, it's going to eat up most of the rest of the morning."

"These things happen," I said. "Listen, I'm not all that far from home, and it's a beautiful morning. Do you mind if I abandon you and walk back for my Jeep?"

"No, I don't mind at all. I'm sorry about this, Suzanne."

"No worries," I said as I patted his cheek. "I need to walk off some of that breakfast anyway. We'll meet up again later."

"How about lunch?" he asked. "We can go back to the Boxcar Grill, unless you're getting tired of it."

"I can't imagine that ever happening," I said with a smile. "I'll wait here with you until you get hold of Momma, and then I'll take off."

"Don't worry about that. If she's not free, I've got half a dozen other folks I can call. Small-town living, right?"

"Right," I said. "Okay then, if you're sure."

"One thing before you go, though," Phillip said in a serious tone.

"What's that?"

"Don't go after Ally or Nathan without me."

"I wouldn't dream of it," I said.

"Promise?"

"I promise," I answered.

"That's good enough for me," he said.

I started off, turning to wave at him as I crossed the street and headed home.

I meant to keep my word to him.

After all, going after a killer alone was not my idea of a good time.

As I walked past Gabby's place, I was surprised to see the front door suddenly open. "Suzanne, what are you doing out walking in front of my house?"

"It's a beautiful day, Gabby, so I thought I'd get a little exercise."

"I've never seen you walk a step out of your way since I've known you. What happened? Did that Jeep of yours finally break down?"

"My Jeep is fine, thank you very much," I said. She was close to the truth, but it was Phillip's vehicle, not mine, that had failed, not that I was going to share that information with her. "How did you happen to see me out here anyway?"

"My doctor has started to insist that I learn to calm myself down," she said. "During my last checkup, he spouted some kind of nonsense that my blood pressure was too high and that I either needed to change my diet, start on medication, learn to meditate, or find some way to change my outlook on life and start letting things slide. Honestly, can you see me doing *any* of those things? Change what I eat? Meditate? Take medicine? I don't think so."

Gabby was high strung and fierce by nature, so it didn't surprise me all that much to learn that her blood pressure was higher than it should have been. "Jake's on medication, and it's helped him quite a bit," I said. I wasn't exactly sharing secrets. Jake made no bones about admitting that he had hypertension.

"Well, it's not for me."

"Gabby, you have to do something. It's dangerous," I said.

"I *am* doing something," she said. "I'm bird watching."

"What? How is that supposed to help you with your high blood pressure?"

"It's intended to calm me down, but I get so aggravated with them that I'm getting worse, not better."

"How can watching birds make you *more* agitated?" I asked her.

"I sit at my window over there," she said as she pointed to the feeders in front of it, "and watch the birds eat. The truth is that it's not very relaxing at all. I've got a mockingbird that hogs the suet, and every time a bluebird tries to come in to eat some, he runs her off."

"You know their sexes?" I asked her, trying to suppress a smile.

"Maybe not, but that's the way they act. Then there's a wren who comes around. Don't get me started on him."

"Let me guess. He's misbehaving, too."

"He grabs, and then throws out, thirty or forty seeds from the feeder until he finds one he likes. I swear sometimes there's a squirrel sitting below him with his mouth open! Then, when the wren's not around, the squirrels climb the pole my feeders are on, and they eat as much as they can stuff into their greedy little cheeks! They're the worst freeloaders of the lot."

She was getting agitated just relaying the story to me, and I worried about her even more. "Clearly feeding the birds isn't the answer for you. Gabby, take the medicine."

"Why should I?" she asked defiantly.

"Because I'd hate for you to have a stroke or a heart attack and die," I said soberly.

"You would? You really would, wouldn't you?" she asked me softly.

"I truly would," I answered.

"Maybe I'll make another appointment with the old gasbag," Gabby said gently. "Oh, I've got good news."

"I'm always in the market for some of that," I said. "What's going on?"

"It turns out that I get to keep every last dime of Lily's insurance money. The money I get isn't a part of her estate at all. I'm going to use most of it to make my shop even better than I'd planned, and I'm going to use the rest of it to take a trip. Isn't that something?"

"It is," I agreed. "I just hate that you had to lose your best friend to do it."

"I do, too," she answered. "Have you made any progress on catching whoever did it?" As Gabby asked me the question, she glanced up and down the street, as though a bad guy might be lurking around the corner, trying to overhear our conversation.

"We are," I admitted.

"Who is it down to?"

"I'm not ready to say that just yet," I hedged.

"Why not?"

"Because I don't want you thinking badly of my suspects when only one of them actually did it," I said. "I've tainted the images of too many people in my mind over the years because of what I've suspected to do that to you."

"It's not an easy thing you do, is it?" Gabby asked me respectfully.

"It can be downright dangerous sometimes," I agreed.

"That's not what I meant. Sure, I know that, too, but I'm talking about the wear and tear on your spirit, Suzanne. Don't you ever think about giving up all this detecting and focusing on your donuts instead?"

"I do, but then I'm not sure I could live with myself knowing that there are killers out there walking around free without paying for what they've done, you know?"

"You could always just leave it to the police," she suggested.

"I could, but there are things I can do, questions I can ask, that they can't. I can push and prod, and most important of all, I can listen. What I do is important." Why was I suddenly defending myself and what I did to Gabby?

"I'm not denying it," she said hastily. She must have realized how what she'd just said had sounded to me. "I for one have been happy to accept your help over the years when I've been in a jam, and I know a lot of folks in town feel the same way. You are honoring Lily by hunting down her killer, and don't think I don't know that. I'm just worried about you," she added as she put a hand on my shoulder. It was a rare moment for Gabby, showing me how she truly felt about me, and it touched me. "You would be missed too, you know."

"Thank you for saying that," I said as I gave her a spontaneous hug.

She seemed to lean into my embrace for a few seconds before she pulled away. "Enough of that. I don't want my neighbors talking."

"I don't care," I said happily. It always made me feel good when someone took the time and the trouble to tell me how they felt about me face to face. Flowers at a funeral were a waste as far as I was concerned. I would rather have a dandelion while I was alive than the most expensive arrangement when I could no longer appreciate it.

"Well, I do," she said as she started back inside.

"Make that appointment," I called out to her.

"Find that killer," she replied.

I was trying to do just that, so there was nothing else I could say.

Chapter 16

AS I GOT CLOSER AND closer to downtown on foot, and to Donut Hearts, I started to wonder about what we knew about our last remaining suspects and how they might be connected with the local Mob. Both seemed like unlikely candidates to be tied in with what passed for organized crime in April Springs. It was hard for me to imagine that there was even such a thing in our small town. Travis had been pretty clear that *someone* had threatened to burn down one of his dry cleaners though, and he'd taken the threat seriously enough to stop his quest to take George's job from him. I had to wonder how that news had sat with Nathan. He'd probably been upset to hear it, especially since he'd been working so hard behind the scenes to make it happen. Was he just doing his job as he saw fit, or did he have another, more powerful motive to want to see George ousted from office? Had he felt the same way about Lily? If he'd wanted her out, couldn't he have just *faked* the results to show that George was the winner? Then again, maybe neither candidate was his idea of an ideal mayor, for whatever reason he might have. By killing Lily and framing George for it, the way would be clear to name Travis mayor. The only problem with that was that Travis clearly wasn't interested in the job, at least not anymore.

Then there was Ally. I had no trouble seeing her connected in some way with bad people. She was notorious for skirting the ethics of her profession to get what she wanted, and there was no love lost between her and Lily. Could she have been trying to pressure the mayor-elect into doing her bidding and gotten pushback or even a flat refusal? Then again, Lily was not only broke but also pretty deep in debt according to all counts, so maybe Ally had tried to use that against her as leverage. Maybe she'd made a run at Lily, trying to force her to do what she wanted, but instead of capitulating, Lily had threatened her. I could see that confrontation happening between the two women, with the disastrous results that had unfolded.

The problem was that they *both* seemed like plausible suspects on the one hand and equally implausible ones on the other.

I didn't know what to think.

I was still pondering the possibilities when a strange vehicle pulled over beside me, and one of my last two suspects said angrily, "Get in the car, Suzanne."

Chapter 17

"NO THANKS. I LIKE walking," I said as I started to move away.

"Do what I tell you, or you're going to regret it," Ally said intently. "I'm not messing around here."

"Ally, are you threatening me?" I asked.

"No, I'm promising you that if you and that washed-up old has-been police chief don't stop digging into Lily Hamilton's murder, you're going to be next."

"That sounds like a threat to me," I said. "Did you kill her, Ally?"

"That's the kind of stupid question you've been asking all over town that has your lives in jeopardy," she said.

"You didn't answer the question," I pushed.

"I'm telling you for the last time. Get in the car!" She was clearly well past just angry now. Her face was flushed, and there was a vein throbbing on her forehead that looked as though it were about to explode.

"No!" I said loudly. I really felt threatened now, and any second, I expected Ally to pull a gun out and try to make me do what she wanted. I'd gotten into a car with a killer before, and it had nearly been the end of me, so one way or the other, this was going to end here and now.

Then I did the only thing I could think to do.

I ran.

Not down the road where she could follow me in her car, but to the nearest house. When no one answered to my frantic pounding, I glanced back to see that Ally had pulled her car over to the shoulder and was getting out.

Was she going to chase me down and shoot me?

I skipped the door and took off through the side yard toward the back.

Fortunately there were no fences, and the yards connected, so I rushed out to the alley in back and ran toward town. Donut Hearts was only a few blocks away, and for some reason, I felt as though it was the only safe place that I could go, all evidence to the contrary. After all, I'd been attacked there in the past, and so had Jake, but it still felt like the only haven on earth to me at the moment.

When I dared to glance back over my shoulder, I didn't see Ally chasing me, or anyone else for that matter.

I still wasn't going to slow down until I'd hit my own home base, though.

Thankfully, the shop was still open, and as I rushed inside, Emma looked up from the counter. "Suzanne, you look as though you've seen a ghost."

"No, it's nothing like that," I said as I finally felt my heartbeat slowing back to its normal speed. "If anybody comes in looking for me, I'm not here, okay?"

"Sure, whatever you say, boss," Emma said, though it was clear she was worried about me and my current state of mind.

That made two of us.

I hurried in back and found Sharon, Emma's mother, washing dishes. "Suzanne? What's up? We didn't expect you in today."

"Like I told Emma, I'm not here. Do you mind taking a break and joining her out front? I need to make a phone call."

"It's your shop," she said with a nod. She hesitated at the door, though. "Is there anything I can do?"

"No, everything's fine," I lied.

Once I was alone, I called my husband. Most folks would have called the police, and technically Jake was working for them at the moment, but I wanted my husband, not just a law enforcement officer. He was the only one who would do.

"Hey, Suzanne, what's up?" he asked the moment he answered my call.

"Jake, I think Ally Tucker killed Lily," I said. Just saying the words made it more real to me somehow.

"So do we," he admitted. "She's not there with you now, is she? Say the word 'probably' like you're answering a question so I'll know that you're in danger."

"She's not here," I said, thinking how clever my husband was to come up with a code word that made perfect sense, as though I were answering a question. "But I saw her on Springs Drive ten minutes ago. She tried to force me into her car."

"What? Are you okay?"

"I'm fine. I ran away like a scared little rabbit," I admitted.

"You did the right thing. Hang on a second. Let me tell Chief Grant." He was gone thirty long seconds, and when he came back on the line, he said, "We've been looking for her. I can't believe she was brazen enough to approach you. Tell me what happened, and don't leave anything out."

I did as he asked, and after I finished, I felt the surge of adrenaline I'd felt earlier fade. "What makes you think she did it, too?"

"We've been looking into her business dealings, and evidently she's been getting some of her projects financed by some pretty shady people. Given what we've been hearing about a criminal element in town behind the murder, it wasn't hard to put it together. We tried to question her this morning, but somehow she got wind of it and ran. Honestly, we figured she'd be out of the state by now. Why did she hang around? Surely not just to threaten you and Phillip."

"Maybe she wanted to clean up a few loose ends before she ran," I said with a shiver. I didn't like the thought of being a loose end for a murderer, but there was nothing I could do about it. "Someone needs to warn Phillip!"

"We'll send someone over to their place right now," Jake said. "Don't worry. He'll be fine."

"He's not at home, though. His truck battery died at Mercy Host's house, and I doubt he and Momma have had time to get it replaced yet."

"Okay. Give me another second." After twenty more beats, he came back on the line. "I just rerouted the officer we dispatched, so Phillip and Dot will have an armed escort until we catch her, and you need one, too."

"Jake, she *already* took a stab at me," I said. "I got away."

"For now," he said, "but I don't like you out running around unprotected."

"I'm perfectly safe here at Donut Hearts," I said.

"Does anyone know that you're there?"

"Just Emma and Sharon," I said. "I'm in the kitchen where no one can see me."

"Okay. Stay there until I can get over there. It might be a while."

"That's fine with me," I said. "I'm in no hurry to be a target for a killer."

"That's my girl," he said, and then he hung up, no doubt to go off in pursuit of Ally Tucker. With any luck, this would all be over before dinnertime tonight, and for once, I didn't have any problem sitting the rest of this case out.

Since I was in the kitchen anyway, I put on my apron, rolled up my sleeves, and finished those dishes that Sharon had started. Not only did they need to be done, but it gave me something to do, something productive, to keep my mind off how close I'd come to being abducted.

Sharon walked back into the kitchen half an hour later. "Suzanne, is your call finished yet? I'm sorry to bother you, but I'd love to finish those dishes... You didn't have to do that."

"I didn't mind," I said. "How are things out front?"

"We're closing in four minutes," she said.

"Sounds good. Do we have many donuts left?"

"Less than a dozen," she admitted. "Why, are you feeling peckish?"

I knew I would be if I had to hide in the back of my shop much longer. "No, I'm good. Has anyone been in asking about me?"

"No, not today," she said, clearly puzzled by my question. "Were you expecting someone?"

"Not today," I answered, mimicking her response to me with a grin.

"Okay then," she said as she rejoined her daughter out front.

I waited five minutes, and then I walked out to join them.

"Are you going to tell us what's going on, or do we have to beg?" Emma asked.

"Jake is hot on the heels of the person who killed Lily, but that's off the record," I added quickly, not wanting either woman to report it to Ray.

"Hey, you know the rule. What happens at Donut Hearts stays at Donut Hearts," Emma said, and Sharon nodded in agreement.

"Thanks," I said as there was a tap at the front door. My heart leapt into my throat as I worried that Ally had tracked me down after all, but to my surprise and delight, it was Jake! "That's my ride," I said as I went to the door to let him in. "Do you two mind if I skip out on you?"

"You were never here to begin with, remember?" Emma asked me.

"I do at that," I said.

I unlocked the door, but instead of letting Jake in, I joined him outside. "I thought you'd never come."

"Sorry, but she's cagier than we realized."

"You haven't caught her yet?" I asked, feeling suddenly tense.

"Not yet. Evidently when you got away from her, she ditched her car, and we have no idea what she's driving now."

"She stole a car?" I asked incredulously. "Why does that surprise me, knowing that she's probably a murderer?"

"That's hard to say, but don't worry. We'll get her."

"Jake, I can't keep myself locked up in the donut shop kitchen while you do. You know that, don't you?"

"Of course I do," he admitted. "Would you settle for going back to the cottage?"

"And hide there?" I asked him incredulously.

"Don't think of it as hiding, Suzanne. Think of it more as though you are just taking some time to relax," he said.

"Sorry, but that's not going to fly, either. Ally has no reason to come after me now. She's running for her life."

"Maybe so, but desperate people do crazy things sometimes," he said.

"Then if that happens, we'll deal with it, but I'm not going to hide anymore." Sitting in the Donut Hearts kitchen waiting for the other shoe to drop had been torture for me. If someone *was* going to come after me, they wouldn't find me cowering in some corner, afraid. I'd be ready to meet them head on, face to face. It might not be the smartest strategy in the world, but earlier, I'd run from Ally like a scared child, and then I'd hidden in my own donut shop kitchen like a quivering mass of jelly, and those things weren't me.

If and when anything else happened in this case, I was going to stand tall and face down whatever came my way.

It was the only way I'd be able to look at myself in the mirror after all of this was over. I wanted my memory of my behavior to be of a strong and capable woman able to handle herself, not some whimpering coward hoping that others would protect me.

It might not be the smartest or most prudent choice, but it was the only one I had, or I would have to quit trying to catch killers altogether.

Chapter 18

"SUZANNE, I DON'T HAVE to go back in if you don't want me to," Jake said later that evening. There was an all-points bulletin out on Ally in four states, but so far, no one had been able to catch a glimpse of her after I'd run away from her. Chief Grant was getting frustrated, and he wanted his so-called brain trust to come in and try to figure out their next move. Not only was Jake involved, but so were Phillip and George Morris, who had himself been a good cop, though it had been a long time ago.

"Go. You can't babysit me for the rest of my life," I told him.

"No, but I can be here until we catch up with Ally."

"What are the odds that she stuck around in April Springs? You know now that she borrowed her assistant's car, and I can't imagine her hanging around just to get back at me. I didn't do anything to the woman."

"Well, you questioned her as a suspect in a murder that she committed. Some folks might think that would be reason enough to get back at you."

"Jake, Phillip and I questioned a handful of people, not just Ally. Sure, she was one of our better suspects, but at one point, we had more than we knew what to do with."

"That may be the case, but she didn't know that," Jake said.

"Would you just go already?" I asked with a smile as I pushed him toward the door.

"Fine, but I won't be long."

"Jake, don't make promises you can't keep. I know how you are when you all get together. It's like a cop's club, and finding Ally is almost an excuse for you all to meet."

"Not for me," he said.

"Maybe not, but the rest of them are counting on you."

"Okay, I'll go, but I'd feel better if Grace or Dot were here with you," Jake said.

"To be honest with you, I don't feel much like company. I'm going to make some popcorn and watch a movie before I go to bed. That's about as exciting as things are going to get around here tonight."

Boy, was I ever wrong.

I just didn't know it at the time.

Chapter 19

I WAS HALFWAY INTO one of my favorite romantic comedies when there was a sudden pounding on my front door. Putting the movie on pause, I grabbed my trusty softball bat and went to the door to see who was so urgently trying to get my attention.

It was Ally Tucker!

I started to pull out my cell phone when she screamed, "Help me! He's right behind me!"

"I'm not letting you in! You killed Lily Hamilton, and I'm not going to let you kill me."

I called Jake, but his phone was busy. I hurriedly hit redial when I saw someone come up out of the bushes and put a hand around Ally's throat.

It was Nathan Billings, and it appeared that we'd all been wrong after all.

"Open up, Suzanne, or she dies right here and now," Nathan said as he squeezed her throat tighter.

I swore that I saw her eyes bulge out a little as he applied more pressure.

"Fine," I said as I put my phone down on the arm of the couch. Maybe the call would go through, and maybe it wouldn't, but I couldn't just leave Ally out there to die at the killer's hand.

I kept the softball bat behind my back, though.

The moment I unlocked the door, Nathan pointed to my bat. "Throw that on the couch."

I'd tried to hide it from him, but clearly I'd failed.

I did as he demanded when his pressure on Ally's throat increased again. Was he going to strangle her right in front of me? "There, are you happy now?"

"I'm nowhere near it, you meddling fool," he said as we stepped inside.

The moment he came into the cottage, he released his grip on Ally's throat, and as he did, he ordered her, "Go get the bat. I don't want her going for it."

I was dumbfounded as she grinned at me. Nathan pulled a gun out and pointed it at me. "I told you that choking you would work better than threatening you with a gun."

"You didn't have to be quite so convincing, though," she said as she rubbed her throat.

"What can I say? I'm a method actor. You knew that when we were in *Othello* together in Maple Hollow."

"You two were in a play together?" I asked them. I'd known about their theater interests, but I'd never put two and two together.

"So was Jimmy Mullins," Nathan said.

"Who's Jimmy Mullins?" I asked numbly.

"She doesn't really know anything, Nathan. This has turned out to be a complete waste of time," Ally said.

"Maybe so, but it's too late for her now," he said.

As he lifted the gun, I tried to stall for more time. "Don't let me die without knowing who Jimmy Mullins is."

"He played the role of the hood who confronted Lily and Travis Johnson," Nathan explained.

"So there's no real organized crime front infiltrating April Springs?"

"It's just the two of us," Nathan said smugly. "I was going to rig the election so Lily would win, and she was supposed to favor us with some influence in getting our developments approved. We all stood to make a fortune, but she suddenly got a case of cold feet on election night, so she had to go."

"You killed her because of a real estate deal?" I asked them both incredulously.

"Don't say it as though it wasn't significant. We were all going to be rich," Ally said.

"Which one of you actually killed her?" I asked.

"Does it matter?" Nathan asked.

"It does to me."

"I swung the ballot box," he said stiffly, "but it was Ally's idea."

"I thought for sure Travis Johnson would cave when Jimmy approached him, but the idiot was too good in the role, and Travis dropped out, too."

"Why didn't you try to pressure George?" I asked, drawing him out as much as I could.

"Everyone knows that George Morris is too scrupulous for his own good," Ally said. She then turned to her coconspirator. "What are you waiting for? Shoot her and let's go."

"Okay, stop pushing me," Nathan complained.

"If I hadn't pushed you into this in the first place, we would have never gotten the chance to make all of that money," she scolded him.

"Some plan. I ended up killing Lily for nothing, now I'm going to do the same to Suzanne, and we still don't have a dime to show for it."

For a moment, they seemed to forget about me as they argued among themselves.

I had one chance, and I decided this was the best, probably even the only opportunity for me to take it.

I raced for the front door, trying to knock Nathan over as I rushed past him. If it had been Ally holding the gun, I probably never would have tried it, but Nathan seemed torn about the prospect of shooting me in cold blood.

At least I hoped so.

And then I heard the gun boom behind me, and a moment later, the bullet whizzed past my ear and embedded itself in the doorframe, shredding the wood where it hit.

So maybe he wasn't all that reluctant after all.

I knew that I couldn't afford to give him a second chance.

I raced outside and into the night, hoping that my knowledge of the woods around my cottage would save me again.

It never came to that, though.

Nathan was raising the gun again as I heard a shot ahead of me, and he crumpled to the ground as he grabbed his leg and screamed in pain.

"Ally's inside," I said, sobbing, as Jake rushed past me to disarm Nathan Billings, and then he plunged inside without any thought for his own safety.

"She's got my softball bat!" I screamed nearly as loudly as Nathan was yelling.

I needn't have worried about my husband. He came out a few moments later with Ally Tucker in tow, and she was now in handcuffs.

At that moment, I heard the sirens roaring up Springs Drive, and I knew that reinforcements would soon be there.

That's when I nearly fainted, but I managed to hold it together long enough to get onto the porch, where I collapsed in a rocker and fought to get my breath back.

It had been too close for comfort. If I hadn't acted, and if Jake hadn't come when he had, I would have been dead, and I knew it.

Chapter 20

"I THOUGHT YOU WERE trained to shoot to kill," I told Jake later at the police station as I sipped a cup of coffee and told my story to him again.

"What can I say? I must be off my game," he answered with a grin.

"I've seen you shoot," I reminded him. "You're as good as you ever were."

"Maybe so, but I've lost my taste for killing," Jake admitted. "I had a good shot at his leg, and besides, I didn't want to miss him and hit you."

"I appreciate that," I said as I reached out and touched his hand.

Chief Grant came in at that moment, noticed that we were having a moment, and then started to step back outside.

"Come on in, Chief," I said as I pulled my hand away. "Is either one of them talking?"

"Are you kidding? I can't get them to shut up," he said as he came all the way in and sat down behind his desk. "Ally was the mastermind, and Nathan was the puppet, at least as far as I've been able to figure out so far. She gave the order that Lily had to die since the development she wanted approved was tied to her, though not Nathan. She lied to him and said that Lily was going to take them both down, so Nathan killed her. They went to a lot of trouble to make sure that Lily won the election, and those missing ballots that Nathan stole proved that George really won the election all along. Who's going to certify it I do not know, but that's not my circus, and it's not my monkeys."

"It was really all about the money?" I asked.

"More like greed," Jake corrected me. "Money isn't inherently evil. After all, even the Bible says that the *love* of money is the root of all evil, not money itself."

"I still can't wrap my head around it," I said. "They both thought I knew more than I really did."

"Suzanne, they fooled everyone, including a handful of trained professionals. If they hadn't been so paranoid about you asking them both so many questions, they might have gotten away with it."

"That makes me feel a little bit better," I said, and then I turned to Chief Grant. "Have you found Jimmy Mullins yet?"

"He was duped," the chief said. "He claims Nathan gave him a hundred bucks each time he threatened someone as a practical joke. Evidently Jimmy loves playing the heavy."

I was about to comment when Momma and Phillip burst in. After Momma hugged me, Phillip said, "I can't believe it was right under our noses the entire time."

"They fooled everybody," I said, "but it was pointed out to me that if we hadn't been pounding our suspects with questions, they might have kept their cool, and then they'd never have gotten caught."

"It's an odd way to close a case out," Phillip said.

"As long as it's closed," I said. It felt good knowing that Lily's killers were going to pay for their crimes.

I was just elated that I hadn't joined her as a victim of those two schemers.

Momma asked Chief Grant, "Do you need them any more tonight?"

"No, we've gotten her statement, so Suzanne and Jake can go."

Suddenly the thought of going back to the cottage where the confrontation had just happened didn't appeal to me at all. How long would it take before I could wipe away the image of that bullet whizzing toward me, and how close it had come to ending my life once and for all?

"Good," she said as she turned to us. "I've been playing with recipes for peanut butter pie that I've been dying to get your opinions on. I hope you two are game for a taste test, because I made three versions."

"I think I can force myself," Jake said with a grin. "What about you, Suzanne?"

"Lead the way," I said.

I knew that I'd eventually get over the traumatic events of that night, but it might take me a while to do it.

In the meantime, I had Jake, Momma, Phillip, and all of the rest of April Springs to make me feel good about being home again.

It was really all that I needed, and I was happy once again that I'd never let greed drive me in my life.

After all, I had more riches than King Midas when it came to the folks who loved me, and that was the only wealth that I'd ever been interested in acquiring.

RECIPES

Momma's Pot Roast

This recipe is one of my slow-cooker favorites. There are variations you can try, say omitting the mushrooms if you'd like, or using full-sodium versions of the broth and soup, but we like this seasoned to the taste of the individual. Lately we've been experimenting with several low-sodium products in the kitchen, and it's amazing to us how much better all of our food tastes. The meat falls apart to the touch, and the veggies are tender. This is a great recipe year round, but we especially enjoy it on a cool autumn evening or a chilly winter afternoon. An added bonus is the house smells delightful as this meal is cooking, and by the time it's complete, I'm always ready to eat!

Ingredients

1 BONELESS BEEF CHUCK roast (2 1/2 to 3 pounds)
- 2 teaspoons seasoning (I like Montreal Steak Seasoning)
- 3 tablespoons flour, all-purpose
- 1/4 cup canola oil, or enough to cover the bottom of your skillet
- 1 can low-sodium fat-free beef broth (14.5 oz.)
- 2 tablespoons butter
- 1 onion, coarsely chopped
- 1 can low-sodium condensed cream of mushroom soup (10 3/4-oz.)
- Baby bella mushrooms, sliced (10 oz.)
- 2 bay leaves
- 1 package baby carrots (16 oz.)
- 6-10 new potatoes (they are small, and we like gold)

Directions

Rub the roast on all sides with the flour mixed with seasoning.

Over medium-high heat, sear the roast on all sides until it's brown in enough canola oil to cover the bottom of your skillet.

Place the roast in the bottom of your slow cooker.

Add the beef broth to the hot pan and deglaze.

Pour the broth onto the meat in the slow cooker. Do not add any water!

In the skillet, melt the butter and sauté half the coarsely chopped onion until it browns slightly.

Spoon out the cream of mushroom soup on top of the roast.

Spoon the sautéed onion on top of the soup, and then add the rest of the onion, coarsely chopped.

Add half the mushrooms, sliced, to the mix.

Add two bay leaves to the mix.

Cook three hours on the High setting.

After three hours, add baby carrots, new potatoes, and the remainder of the mushrooms (sliced) to the mix. An alternative is to add the potatoes after three hours and the carrots and mushrooms after two, but either way is fine.

Continue cooking for three hours on High, and then enjoy!

One option is to make gravy by adding cornstarch to the juices after cooking and reducing the result to half on the stovetop by simmering it.

Yields 4 to 6 servings.

Delightful Pineapple Upside-Down Cake

This is one of our favorite treats in my household, and cast iron is the perfect cookware for it. I don't normally make it outside in my firepit, but I know that some folks bake this treat in a Dutch oven over the coals. Wherever you prepare it, it's absolutely delicious. We all love to eat it fresh from the oven, when the pineapple slices and the cherries are both still warm from baking, though some members of my family like it better the next day after it's been in the fridge. As for me, I refuse to choose, sampling some on both days. I wish I could tell you what it tastes like the day after that, but we've never had one last that long. One member of my family even insists on this as a birthday cake substitute, it's so delicious!

Ingredients

Topping (actually the base, as it is being prepared)

1/3 cup butter, melted

1/2 cup light brown sugar, packed

1 can sliced pineapple, drained (8.25 oz.)

Maraschino cherries (as needed)

Cake

1 1/2 cups cake flour

1 cup granulated sugar

3/4 cup milk (whole or 2%)

1/3 cup shortening

1 egg, beaten

2 teaspoons baking powder

1 1/2 teaspoons vanilla

1/2 teaspoon table salt

Directions

Preheat the oven to 350°F.

Make the topping first. On the stovetop, melt the butter in a nine-inch cast iron skillet over low heat. Sprinkle the brown sugar over the melted butter. Then place the pineapple slices around the bottom of the pan, putting one in the center of the skillet for presentation. Cut as needed to fit the bottom. Then place cherries in the centers and curves of the pineapple slices. Remove the skillet from the heat and set aside.

In a large mixing bowl, combine the flour, sugar, milk, shortening, egg, baking powder, vanilla, and salt at a low speed with a hand mixer or stand mixer, scraping constantly for 30 seconds. Then beat on high, scraping occasionally, for 2 to 3 minutes, until the ingredients are combined. Pour the batter evenly over the fruit in the cast iron skillet bottom.

Bake until a toothpick inserted in the center comes out clean, approximately 20 to 30 minutes, depending on your oven and skillet. Invert onto a heat-proof plate and let the skillet remain in place for a few minutes. Remove it carefully and then serve while it's still warm.

Yields 6 to 8 servings.

Suzanne's Apple Fritters

I'm a huge fan of apple fritters, and there's nothing quite like the taste of homemade. I have them dusted with powdered sugar, full-on glazed with my usual donut glaze mix of powdered sugar and water, but some folks like to dip these in some apple butter for a double whammy!

Ingredients

3/4 cup all-purpose flour

1/4 cup sugar (white)

1 tablespoon baking powder

1 tablespoon cinnamon

1/3 cup milk (2% or whole)

1/4 teaspoon salt

1 egg, beaten

1/2 cup chopped apple (something tart; I like Granny Smiths for this)

Directions

Heat canola oil for frying to 360°F while you mix the batter.

Sift the dry ingredients, then stir in milk and beaten egg. Fold in the chopped apple, and then take a teaspoon of batter and rake it into the fryer with another spoon. If the dough doesn't rise to the top of the oil soon, gently nudge it with a chopstick, being careful not to splatter oil. After 2 minutes, check, and then flip, frying for another minute on the other side. These times may vary given too many factors to count, so keep a close eye on the fritters.

Makes about a dozen small fritters.

The World's Best Pumpkin Donuts

Like Suzanne, sometimes I make these delightful treats in the heat of summer. While they are expected in the fall and winter months, there's nothing like the taste of autumn when it's sweltering outside here in North Carolina. The flavors are subtle, and if you want to enhance them, you can always increase the spices you use in the blend, but no matter how you make them, find a way that you enjoy and then go for it!

Ingredients
2 eggs, beaten
1 cup sugar
2 tablespoons canola oil
1 can pumpkin puree (16 oz.)
2/3 cup buttermilk
4–5 cups bread flour
4 teaspoons baking powder
1/2 teaspoon baking soda
1 teaspoon salt
1 teaspoon nutmeg
1 teaspoon cinnamon
1/2 teaspoon ground ginger
Directions

In a large mixing bowl, beat the eggs thoroughly and then add the recommended amount of sugar, mixing until it's all incorporated. Next add the oil, pumpkin, and buttermilk, then mix it all together again.

In a separate bowl, combine all of the dry ingredients, holding back 1 cup of the flour, mixing 4 cups of flour, the baking powder, baking soda, salt, nutmeg, cinnamon, and ground ginger. Sift the dry ingredients together and then add them slowly to the egg mix.

Once you've got them well mixed, chill the dough for about an hour.

When the dough is thoroughly chilled, roll it out on a floured surface until it's about 1/4 inch thick, then cut out donuts and holes with your donut cutter. While the donuts are resting, heat the oil in your fryer to 375°F. Add the donuts to the oil a few at a time, turning them once after a couple of minutes.

Take them out, drain them on a rack, then they're ready to eat. These are good with powdered sugar on top or just plain.

Makes approximately 1 dozen donuts.

If you enjoy Jessica Beck Mysteries and you would like to be notified when the next book is being released, please visit our website at jessicabeckmysteries.net for valuable information about Jessica's books, and sign up for her new-releases-only mail blast.

Your email address will not be shared, sold, bartered, traded, broadcast, or disclosed in any way. There will be no spam from us, just a friendly reminder when the latest book is being released, and of course, you can drop out at any time.

Other Books by Jessica Beck

The Donut Mysteries
Glazed Murder
Fatally Frosted
Sinister Sprinkles
Evil Éclairs
Tragic Toppings
Killer Crullers
Drop Dead Chocolate
Powdered Peril
Illegally Iced
Deadly Donuts
Assault and Batter
Sweet Suspects
Deep Fried Homicide
Custard Crime
Lemon Larceny
Bad Bites
Old Fashioned Crooks
Dangerous Dough
Troubled Treats
Sugar Coated Sins
Criminal Crumbs
Vanilla Vices
Raspberry Revenge
Fugitive Filling
Devil's Food Defense
Pumpkin Pleas
Floured Felonies
Mixed Malice

Tasty Trials
Baked Books
Cranberry Crimes
Boston Cream Bribes
Cherry Filled Charges
Scary Sweets
Cocoa Crush
Pastry Penalties
Apple Stuffed Alibies
Perjury Proof
Caramel Canvas
Dark Drizzles
Counterfeit Confections
Measured Mayhem
Blended Bribes
Sifted Sentences
Dusted Discoveries
Nasty Knead
Rigged Rising
The Classic Diner Mysteries
A Chili Death
A Deadly Beef
A Killer Cake
A Baked Ham
A Bad Egg
A Real Pickle
A Burned Biscuit
The Ghost Cat Cozy Mysteries
Ghost Cat: Midnight Paws
Ghost Cat 2: Bid for Midnight
The Cast Iron Cooking Mysteries
Cast Iron Will

Cast Iron Conviction
Cast Iron Alibi
Cast Iron Motive
Cast Iron Suspicion
Nonfiction
The Donut Mysteries Cookbook

Manufactured by Amazon.ca
Bolton, ON